Thalia Poser

*A Tale of Faith, Family, and Friendship
in an Appalachian Mining Town*

Harold Voyles

Trilogy Christian Publishers
A Wholly Owned Subsidary of Trinity Broadcasting Network
2442 Michelle Drive
Tustin, CA 92780

Cover design by: Cornerstone Creative Solutions

For information, address Trilogy Christian Publishing
Rights Department, 2442 Michelle Drive, Tustin, Ca 92780.
Trilogy Christian Publishing/ TBN and colophon are trademarks of Trinity Broadcasting Network.

For information about special discounts for bulk purchases, please contact Trilogy Christian Publishing.

Manufactured in the United States of America

Trilogy Disclaimer: The views and content expressed in this book are those of the author and may not necessarily reflect the views and doctrine of Trilogy Christian Publishing or the Trinity Broadcasting Network.

10 9 8 7 6 5 4 3 2 1

Library of Congress Cataloging-in-Publication Data is available.

ISBN 978-1-63769-142-7 (Print Book)
ISBN 978-1-63769-143-4 (ebook)

Dedication

Thalia Poser is dedicated to my wife, Merida, whose encouragement and faith are unending.

Preface

In 1984, I left Kentucky for Fernandina Beach, Florida. I was a thirty-five-year-old coal miner from Harlan County and had grown weary of the mining industry's boom and bust cycle. Yet, I always returned to the coalfields believing that good times were back for good.

A decade later, I returned home for a family reunion. Back in the hills once again, I began to look at my life differently. Although my family had endured hardships, there was much good about Appalachia that I had forgotten.

As I listened to my aunts and uncles recall stories from their past, I realized that I had lacked nothing in my youth but material things. I had forgotten how important faith, family, and friendship were to the people of the region.

I decided right then to write about Appalachia. I first published a book of poetry, *Appalachian Sketches,* and later a play about an Appalachian mountain preacher, *Shadow of a Man.* In 2018, I published *Crooked Creek*, a novel that was loosely based on my life as a coal miner in Harlan County, Kentucky.

A year ago, I began writing a short novel about an Appalachian mountain preacher titled *Jesse Collins.* As the novel progressed, the female character, Thalia Poser, began to assert herself. Thalia reminded me of my strong-willed, physically tough aunts who were raised in mining camps.

Somewhere along the way, Thalia took over, and I just went along for the ride.

Although the hardship of coal miners has been well-documented over the years, women like Thalia Poser have passed under the radar. With all due respect to Jesse Collins, it is only right that the novel bear Thalia's name.

Introduction

Thalia Poser is a story about a family in the Appalachian coal-fields of eastern Kentucky in 1960. The story chronicles the family's dreams and struggles as they try to adapt to a changing way of life.

Thalia, forty-three, is a lanky, tomboyish, yet attractive woman who can express herself only through drawing and painting. Will, her preoccupied and insensitive husband, is unaware of Thalia's needs and is baffled by her unusual physical strength, resulting from her years of hard labor. Thalia uses her keen wit and sharp tongue as a shield while yearning to share her dreams with someone capable of understanding her.

Meanwhile, Jesse Collins, a coal miner turned preacher, complicates Thalia's life. Jesse is Thalia's former fiancé and carries the dual burden of pastoring a hard-headed flock while trying to maintain a friendship with Thalia without crossing a line.

Thalia and her family dwell in a log cabin located on twenty-five acres up an isolated hollow. A large coal company arrives on the scene and promises the idle miners jobs if the mountain families sell their land. The company covets the Poser property because of its ideal location. Will intends to sell the family's property and abandon a way of life that has survived for generations.

The Posers' son, Ollie, has an almost fanatical attachment to their land and believes coal mining will destroy the environment and their way of life. When Ollie discovers his father's deception, he goes on a rampage that leads to tragedy.

Chapter One

A speck of light sneaked past the window shade and the heavy curtains in the bedroom that had only one window. But it was enough light to awaken Thalia Poser. She glanced at Will, her husband of twenty-three years, whose name had been mercifully shortened from Wilberforce. The name was instrumental in Will getting into a half-dozen fistfights as a youth. But when he turned sixteen and suddenly developed an interest in girls, he somehow managed to turn the awkward name into a positive. Girls called him Wilberforce and smiled and giggled to let him know they were interested.

This morning, Thalia was more tired than when she went to bed. And Will did not help. Thankfully, he stopped snoring around two-thirty after she shook him hard enough to awaken someone from a moonshine drunk. Now, he was gently snoring again.

It was a few minutes after six, and Will had said he wanted up at the crack of dawn. Should she wake him? Thalia stared at his ruggedly handsome face with its three days growth of whiskers. When she gently touched his beard, he squirmed, and she jerked her hand away. She slowly eased from the bed and, without looking, slid her feet into fur-lined slippers.

She padded her big feet, too big for a woman, Will liked to say, across the hard pine plank floors. She winced when the boards squeaked. She wanted at least an hour of silence before Will came pounding through the kitchen and asking, "What's for breakfast?"

Their 1,600-square-foot cabin squatted atop a hill, up a hollow, overlooking twenty-five acres of farmland and forest. Thalia looked out the window at an almost empty Hummingbird feeder. Thalia thought the birds had gone south for the winter because she had not seen one in weeks.

Thalia had grown weary of mixing sugar water for the Hummingbirds and bought some from a local feed and grain store in Hoedown, a small mining town two miles away. The Hummingbirds would not touch it. Was it because of the red color, or did it have a different taste? All she knew was that her Hummingbirds were picky.

The oversized kitchen was blessed with three large windows yielding a view of the valley below. Thalia considered the kitchen her domain and defended the territory with the diligence of a German Shepherd guarding a backyard. When the cabin was built thirteen years ago, Will and Thalia repeatedly battled over the number of windows a kitchen needed. "I'll build it the way I see fit," Will had declared. "Three windows is a waste of money. Besides, they're drafty and will make it harder to keep the cabin warm."

"I'll catch you gone on one of your mysterious fishing trips, and your son and I will install the windows," Thalia had replied. Thirteen years later, Thalia looked out her three windows and saw the Hummingbird feeder swaying in the wind. The Almanac said it would be a bitter winter. Although it was only the first day of November, Thalia was already dreading the cold.

After drinking a second cup of coffee, she picked up a pin and ink drawing that she had struggled with for two days. The drawing looked suspiciously like Ollie, her son, who would be seventeen in nine months. Ollie quit high school a month ago, although his grades were decent—two B's and three C's.

Will was so angry he went to town and got drunk. But every time Thalia turned around, Will was getting mad and getting drunk. Thalia thought Will was a fragile vessel sitting too close to the edge of a fireplace mantle, and it would take little to topple him.

If she burned the cornbread or put vanilla icing instead of chocolate on a cake, he went to town. One Saturday afternoon, he was listening to a college basketball game on the radio when the batteries weakened and propelled him into a foul mood.

"If Kentucky wins, you celebrate and get drunk. If they lose, you drown your sorrows by getting drunk. You've got all the bases covered, haven't you," Thalia said in her half-mocking voice. Her teasing irritated Will so much, he often deemed it another reason to get drunk.

The wind picked up, and Thalia felt a slight draft coming through the middle window. She would have Ollie fix it. He loved working with his hands, especially doing woodwork. Ollie would do anything his mother asked, but if Will asked him to bring in a few logs or a bucket of coal for the fireplace, the fur would fly. They seldom ate supper without an argument ensuing. Ollie had finally agreed to return to school in January, so maybe things would get better.

After thirty minutes, Thalia finished the drawing and put it aside. Maybe she could work on it later. Thalia picked up another, almost finished, picture. The drawing was of a short, wide-shouldered, powerful-looking man a little older than her age of forty-three.

His face was a half-smile that hinted of sadness. Thalia had erased his eyes and was redoing them, so they shone with a light whose source was easy to imagine. After she finished the drawing, she held it near the lantern for a long time. When a cloud passed by the windows, darkening the room, she quickly stuffed the picture in her art book.

Thalia saw a blur of something outside her window. She ran to the sink and saw a Hummingbird. What was it doing this far north in November? The Hummingbird plunged his beak in the nectar holder for a couple of sips as if trying to decide if the food might be better elsewhere. Suddenly, it darted away.

Thalia moved quickly and gracefully to the stove on long athlete's legs, muscular from riding horses so much over the years. She was a little too tall to suit most men. Thalia wondered if that was part of Will's problem. *If so, too bad,* Thalia said to herself. She was not going to shrink just to make her husband feel at ease. Besides, Thalia thought he was incapable of being content, much less happy. Thalia considered contentment a more realistic goal to pursue.

Nor did Thalia have patience with people who said they were unhappy. It was an expression people used who did not necessarily like themselves. When things did not suit them, they could blame their husbands, wives, children, or even the governor.

Thalia smiled as she threw some kindling in the kitchen's coal stove and lighted crumpled newspaper beneath it. Soon a fire would be blazing. Thalia started rattling the pots and pans loud enough to wake the neighbors in the next hollow. She wondered how she could be so happy and sad at the same time.

A half-hour later, Thalia sensed the presence of someone in the room. When she turned around, Will was sitting at the kitchen table. She filled his favorite coffee mug too full, and some sloshed on the table. He took several sips and set the coffee mug down hard.

"You're welcome," she said and began humming a tune as she fixed biscuits from scratch. It was a Saturday morning ritual for the Poser family. Gravy and biscuits, sausage, and fried apples. There were six apple trees in the yard, and they were so productive Thalia could not get rid of the apples. Although Thalia baked two apple pies every week, and Ollie gave the horses apples for desert, they seemed to multiply.

Finally, Will spoke. Sadness hovered about Will as if the blues had saturated his clothes. In the past, Thalia tried repeatedly to get him to talk. Talk about anything. But just when he would open up a little, he would stop, reverse directions, and withdraw even further. One day Thalia awoke and decided it was not worth the effort. And somewhere along the way, Thalia preferred that he not talk at all.

Thalia began to hum loudly without realizing it. "What's that dang song you're always humming? Why don't you go ahead and sing?" Will grumbled.

"I will when I get tired of humming."

"For some reason, that tune sticks in my head and drives me crazy."

"It's a short trip for some folks."

"What's that supposed to mean?"

Thalia did not reply as she cut the dough into strips and placed layers over a deep dish filled with apples. She looked out the window at the hill below and absentmindedly ran a hand through her hair to pat back a loose strand. She opened the oven door and shoved the dish inside the woodburning cookstove before slamming the door and quickly jerking her hands away.

She again looked out the windows as if searching for something on the distant horizon. Perhaps she was recalling a memory from long ago, or a forgotten humorous tale, or summoning up an image of someone who was once dear to her but now lost. Gradually, a smile blanketed her face. She stood erect and gracefully spun around to face Will.

"Thalia, you're pretty, but you look kind of like a man from the back, wearing that dang flannel shirt. You look like a lumberjack."

"When you compliment me, you always manage to take half of it back. You knew I was five-eight when you married me."

"It's not that. It's just you're so darn strong for a woman. It doesn't seem right."

Why did everything Will say irritate her? She was raised with four brothers and had to work the fields the same as they did. She played baseball in a deserted cornfield and could outhit two brothers. She had been expected to chop her share of kindling and occasionally saw logs. It was the life they lived, and she had loved it. And she had felt loved. And she sure as heck was not going to apologize for being blessed with physical strength.

It did not take Will long to figure out he had said the wrong thing again and hastily changed the subject. "We should be able to get electricity in Fancy Hollow in four months. They've already started to run the power lines up Wooten Hollow, and that place is half shacks. We'll get us an oil furnace and not have to burn coal. No more kerosene lamps or candles."

"You can't be coal for heat, and I love burning candles."

"How'd this place get named Fancy Hollow? Ain't nothing fancy about it."

Thalia's dad, Walter Thacker, inherited eleven acres from his grandfather and named it after his first sweetheart. Walter thought the name Fancy suited the petite and excitable girl. But Fancy's parents said she had to complete two years of high school or reach age seventeen before she could marry.

Fancy died from a rare summer flu a month after completing tenth grade. Thalia was sure she had told the story to Will a half-dozen times.

"I can't believe I don't remember Fancy's last name. But daddy said he only kissed two women in his whole life— Fancy and Momma."

"Lord, Thalia. You're what forty-two, forty-three, and still call him daddy? I don't get it."

"There's a lot you don't get. I was a daddy's girl. Daddy said if I'd been a boy, I could have whipped George and Troy. They were the oldest. I could hold my own with Truman, and I could whip Milton until he turned fourteen."

"Your brothers would rather fight than eat a two-inch-thick steak. If George and Troy worked at a job like they did the fighting, they'd had more money than a bluegrass lawyer."

"We were a loving family, but my brothers loved to play pranks. One Halloween night, they toppled fourteen out-houses in Hoedown. They claimed it was a record."

"Your family never did have much to brag about. But they sure spoiled you. I made you cry that time we broke up for a week. Truman and George caught me down at the company store one day. They said if I ever made you cry again, I better light out for Detroit."

"Maybe you'd been better off if you'd went to Detroit."

Will stood suddenly and began pacing the floor. The Poser's never received Friday's mail. If Doak Owens, the mail carrier, was a half-hour late, Will felt like the Postal Service should fire him. Doak had been suspended twice over the years, and it seemed to make him even slower. People said Doak would stop and chat with a tree stump.

Will suddenly stopped, yanked open the back door, and pitched his coffee on the ground, and slammed the mug on the table. "I'm going to the post office. I'm expecting an important letter. If Doak gets here, put the letter up. I don't want nobody reading my personal mail."

"You're not going to wait for breakfast? The biscuits are almost done."

"Let Ollie and my dad eat it all. They can eat more than a pack of stray dogs."

When Will reopened the door to leave, Thalia began to sing loudly and slightly off-key. Will's shoulders hunched as the lyrics bullied him off the porch and down the steps on the way to his truck.

Whenever I hear the church bells ring,
Oh, my spirit soars, and I joyfully sing

Chapter Two

Will's truck sputtered down the washboard path that was called a road only because it led out of Fancy Hollow. Thalia retrieved the drawing with troubling eyes and stared at it for a long time. Somehow it seemed incomplete. Something was missing.

Strange how Thalia loved to draw and paint but was never quite satisfied with any of her creations. Years ago, Thalia would show a drawing to Will and ask him for an opinion. The best compliment she hoped to receive was "it's not too bad," or maybe just a grunt of approval. Now, she no longer showed him anything. More often than not, Thalia hid something from him. But this particular drawing was something she definitely did not want him to see.

Her brain began to itch. It was not the eyes but the smile. The smile hinted at submerged grief, barely contained. It was more a grin than a smile, somehow suggesting a combination of merriment and mischief. She would finish it later, after Ollie and Hankins, Will's dad, got up and ate breakfast. Thalia could hear Hankins snoring through the thick log walls of his bedroom. She smiled.

Later in the day, for the third time, Thalia retrieved her rough drawing and vowed to make it right. Ollie had ridden his horse to the far end of their twenty-five acres to select trees for cutting. The local coal company had opened a new section, hired twenty-five miners, and needed more timbers for roof support.

After Hankins helped Thalia clean up the kitchen, he limped to the front porch, smoked his pipe, and waited for a mining buddy to take him to town. Hankins had been retired for six years, and despite failing health, which seemed to strike all coal miners six months after they quit work, he was determined to fight the good fight. He was always saying, "I ain't got much to do, but I keep doing it just the same."

Thalia thanked God for her father-in-law. He had the gift of finding some good in everything. She laughed when she recalled how Hankins and Ollie beamed with pride after they had dug a pit to relocate the outhouse. Hankins was as proud as if he had picked the winning horse in the Kentucky Derby.

It was a little past noon when Thalia was sitting at the kitchen table with a mug of coffee and a large art book. An assortment of artist's brushes and paints and pens were relaxing next to a sketching pad. When someone knocked on the door, Thalia jarred the table, and dots of ink leaped on the sketching pad. Thalia muttered under her breath and yelled for the visitor to enter.

A short, stocky man, a few inches taller than Thalia, stepped through the door, swiping at his coat. It was spitting snow. Pastor Jesse Collins smiled broadly but moved cautiously as if each step had been pre-determined. His appearance was similar to the pen and ink drawing that Thalia had struggled to finish earlier in the day. The grin on the man's face definitely belonged to the drawing.

When Thalia saw Jesse, she threw back her shoulders, raised her head, and brightened the cabin with her smile. "Pastor, if it's not too much trouble, would you mind shutting the door?"

"Glad to, Mrs. Poser."

"Jesse, what are you up to besides pestering the devil?"

"I just got back from a revival this week. You remember that time we went to a revival over in Harlan. They said that preacher was a snake-handler. We joked that if I ever preached, I'd never handle snakes. But who'd ever thought I'd become a man of the Bible?"

"Not me, for sure."

"I can't believe it's spitting snow the first day of November."

"It's the second. It's a wonder you know when to show up for church."

"I forgot a Wednesday night service my first year, and Deacon Cartwright wanted to run me off. I'd probably been better off if he had."

"You almost split the church down the middle that time when you shoved him up against a wall. Did they teach you that in seminary?"

Even though it happened eight years ago, Jesse still grimaced when he thought about what he had done. How could he lose his temper like that? Hawthorne Cartwright had been a thorn in the side of every pastor at the little church. And Cartwright had never liked Jesse from the beginning. But, as he recalled, neither did Thalia's father. Her father had repeatedly told Thalia that Jesse Collins loved to drink and fight and would never amount to a hill of beans. After Jesse left Kentucky a second time, Walter Thacker told Thalia, "What'd I tell you about him? If Jesse cared about you, he would've stayed. But he ran off like a third grader getting clear of a playground bully."

"Mrs. Poser, I shouldn't be here. I came to see Will."

"Pastor, I have a first name, and you should know it by now."

After all the years, Thalia had never asked Jesse why he left without saying goodbye. But she did not have to ask. They had planned to wed as soon as Jesse paid for the five acres that old rascal Horton Spencer promised to sell him. Spencer said he would give Jesse four months to come up with the money.

While Jesse was working in a foundry in Cleveland and trying to save every nickel he earned, Spencer sold the property for a few hundred dollars more. Jesse returned home after losing twenty pounds but gaining a hatful of hundred dollars bills. Jesse was so proud he could bust. On the way home, Jesse stopped in Hoedown at a local bar to make a phone call. He overheard the bartender tell someone that the Johnson boys were bragging that old man Spencer sold them five of the prettiest acres a man ever did see.

If Jesse had not been drunk that night and got his truck stuck in a ditch, he would be sitting in prison today. He would have shot Spencer dead. But that was long before Jesse started preaching.

Suddenly, Thalia blurted out, "Jesse, why did you leave without saying goodbye? Why?"

"Mrs. Poser, you're starting a conversation in the middle of something. You mean, years ago?"

"You left without saying goodbye and stayed gone three years. There was other land you could've bought for us."

"Mrs. Poser, I mean Thalia, your family always had property. Can you imagine how important owning land was to a poor boy like me that never had much of nothing?"

"We thought you were dead."

After more than twenty years, how could he tell Thalia the real reason he left the second time? She was right in a way; he had been dead. He went back to Cleveland, then Detroit, before moving on to Chicago, where he got a job in a foundry and stayed fourteen months. Although he earned good wages, he stayed holed up in a rented room on the fourth floor and hardly got out. He figured if he had stayed much longer, he would never have left his room even to go to work.

Jesse had made plenty of friends in Cleveland and Detroit and courted a lot of pretty girls. The girls, especially in Detroit, were enchanted by his hillbilly accent. But one day, he awoke at dawn, packed his two suitcases, and caught a Trailways bus to Chicago.

He got another job in another foundry and rented another room. But this time, something had changed. He started dreaming of Kentucky at least once a week—always a variation of the same theme. He would lie awake half the night, counting lost days, instead of counting sheep.

He stayed stay home on Saturday night and propped his feet on the windowsill and watched the pavement cool. It was so hot it felt like the streets hated him and wanted him to die. When fall arrived, Jesse opened his windows and swore he could smell the woodfires burning back home. Jesse missed October in the mountains so bad he could hardly stand it.

Jesse had even stopped going to church—something he had done most of his life. However, on most Sunday evenings, he would sit on a church's steps and listen to the singing and preaching. If someone came out to invite him inside, he would apologize and find another church the next Sunday until it happened again. Why did his faith that once gave him joy now cause him pain? Jesse figured if his mom had not died, he would still be in Chicago looking out that window.

"I need to go. I thought Will was here, and I wanted to talk to him. He's got a good head for business."

"You're the pastor visiting his flock. Nothing wrong with that."

"You haven't been to church in eight months."

"The last time I was there, you kept losing your train of thought. Cartwright told the other deacons he never got a thing out of the message. I thought I did you a favor by staying away."

"You sat in the first row. You could have set farther back. Thalia, I'm sorry, but I need to go."

"Stay awhile. I fixed a fresh pot of coffee, and the apple pie is ready."

When Jesse finished his pie and coffee, he scooted his chair close to Thalia and looked at her drawing. She was sketching him. Jesse started to brush a strand of hair back from her face, but a cloud passed by the window freeing the sun. His shadow was cast upon the wall, revealing a twisted, grotesque replica of himself. He jerked his hand away.

Thalia folded the sketch of Jesse twice and handed it to him. He put it in his shirt pocket and patted his heart. Thalia smiled.

"Jesse, don't you get lonely? Don't you have someone?"

"It's been two years, but it's worse at Christmas. You'd think I'd overcome it being a preacher. The fact is, I'm no different from Will or anyone else. I guess when you're alone too long, you start dying a little at a time. The problem is everybody knows it but you."

"You're nothing like Will. Never say you're like Will again."

Could he explain how he felt to Thalia? It seemed like he had always made the wrong move. Jesse believed if it were raining ham sandwiches, he would be inside taking a nap on the couch. But lately, things had gotten worse. Sometimes, Jesse felt there were two of him. And when he was standing still, he thought he could see his shadow move, as if it had a will of its own.

"Thalia, I'm going now."

"Can you come to supper sometime? It's better to talk to Will after he's had a good fried chicken dinner."

"I like fried chicken."

"I wouldn't trust a preacher who didn't eat fried chicken."

"Thalia, you're something else."

"Jesse, I'm worried about you because something is wrong."

"Yeah, but it's kind of hard to explain. It's like, well, one day working underground, I walked past this transformer where a 7,200-volt cable was connected to the back. The cable had a small cut in it, and it took all my strength to pull away from it. I was so weak I had to sit down and rest. A few minutes later, that cable blew. You wouldn't believe the noise. The electrician said I was lucky to be alive."

"The Lord was looking out for you."

"But Thalia, the weird thing was I wanted to give in to that pull. That's the way I feel now. I'm being drawn toward something that I fear yet long for. It's like there's something I'm meant to do, and time is getting short."

"You've been preaching in the Old Testament again. When you preach about Jesus, you light up like a lantern on a moonless night."

Suddenly Thalia clasped Jesse's hand and held it tight. Thalia's strength surprised Jesse when he tried to pull his hand away.

"Thalia, please."

"Jesse, Jesse, Jesse."

"I'm going now. Right now."

Thalia released Jesse's hand, and they both bowed their heads.

Chapter Three

Ollie Poser was built close to the ground, square-headed, and tagged with a country-boy ruggedness. Although he had the same dark curly hair and olive skin as his mother, he did not look quite like either parent. But Ollie's smile belonged to his mother and was so deeply etched on his face it appeared unremovable.

Ollie swaggered through the cabin door, exhibiting the joy and excitement of youth that was often displayed unconvincing by adults. With the door opened wide, and the heat fleeing, Ollie removed his muddy boots and placed them outside. The last time he tracked mud across Thalia's freshly-mopped floor, she said he could not eat a bite until he cleaned up the mess. Ollie had thought about grumbling until he realized a platter of fried pork chops was calling to him from the table.

Although Thalia spoke softly, even when angry, there was something in her voice that said not to cross a line with her. But even when Thalia was angry, he could sense love in everything she touched. He sometimes wondered if loving so much was a good thing. But with his dad, well, that was a different matter. Ollie loved Will Poser but did not like him all that much.

Will blew a gasket when he found out Ollie had quit school. His dad thought it was for fighting, but Thalia later informed Will there was more to the story. When Ollie had something to tell his dad, he often had Thalia relay the message. It seemed to work better that way. Ollie had read little over the years and experienced even less. Consequently, Ollie viewed life through a dark window, and occasionally, life was a blur. But not right now.

Ollie dreamed one day of building a small cabin far away from everyone and everything. He tried to imagine how it would be. He could see himself coming home from a day in the woods and a pretty wife waiting for him, wearing an apron with a dusting of flour, handing him a steaming mug of coffee while he rested, knowing that a good supper awaited him. His wife would be playful and affectionate, and he would bask in the warmth and glory of her love.

He tried hard to conjure up a potential wife's face, but his inexperience distorted the vision. So far, there had only been two girls in his life—Jenny and Cindy—but nothing much came of it. When he talked about farming, hunting, or logging, Jenny rolled her eyes, and Cindy smiled. He knew that rolling eyes was a coward's way of imparting an insult, but Cindy's smile remained a mystery. She had said the Poser cabin was beautiful. Maybe he would give her another chance.

Ollie knew he had fumbled the opportunity to express what he felt. But he figured it would gradually come to him. Maybe he could talk to his granddad about it. His granddad had been around. From the stories Hankins often told, he had been around a little too much.

So far, it had been a good day. Ollie had been out marking trees to cut for a coal company. He loved it. The company was always trying to save a nickel on timbers, but he had driven a hard bargain. Ollie wanted to talk his dad into letting him clear more trees. That way, he could buy a tractor, and, instead of just a family garden, Ollie could farm the land.

They had twenty-five acres, and at least ten acres were suitable for farming. It would work if Ollie could just convince his dad. That would be the hard part. They had hardly talked since Ollie quit school. Ollie wished he could relate to his dad like he could to his granddad, Will's dad.

Thinking of his granddad must have telegraphed a message to Hankins Poser because he immediately opened his bedroom door that faced the kitchen. Wearing overalls latched on one side, Hankins, who looked like a worn-out version of Ollie, had the body of a much younger man. Yet he wore the face of someone who had collected a social security check for a decade.

Hankins moved with an energized stoop as his twinkling eyes revealed a yearning to tease. Hankins ran both hands inside his denim overalls and scratched joyfully, causing Ollie to roar with laughter. They both grabbed a mug of coffee and sat down at the kitchen table at the same time.

"Apple pie. I could smell it when I stepped on the front porch," Ollie said.

"Your mom's been cooking all day. There's cornbread, beans, and fried potatoes on the stove, waiting on a hungry boy to eat it."

"I'm hungry and cold too. It's spitting snow, and that's unusual for early November."

"I remember when I was in fourth grade, or was it the fifth? Anyway, it snowed so deep one November I stayed in the house for three days. We cleared a path to the barn and outhouse, and that was it. Mom had to switch me and Coy, my brother, every day for fighting. I guess we got on each other's nerves pretty bad."

Ollie grinned and fought back a chuckle. "Granddad, how come it rained more, snowed more, and got hotter when you were a kid?"

"Seemed that way to me. I swear, I'm itching to death. Reckon your mom has changed brands of washing powders? One that smells the best itches me the most."

"You're getting old."

"Been old a long time. I remember my momma, God rest her soul, always saying she was tired of being tired. Didn't know what she meant then, but I do now."

"Is your arthritis acting up? They say the hot weather in Florida is good for arthritis."

Hankins stopped talking long enough to light his pipe. Years ago, Hankins and two friends talked about buying a fishing boat and going shrimping in Florida. Every time one or the other had a sharp pain in the knee, back, or hip, they revived the subject. But they would never leave the hills of Kentucky.

One friend, Chester Wiggins, had left Kentucky on several occasions. But Herman McKnight, the other friend, had seldom been more than a hundred miles from where he was born and raised. Still, it was fun to dream. It did not cost a lot unless it made you unhappy with what you had and where you were.

Hankins could remember when he left home looking for work because the coal mine had reduced the workforce or completely shut down. Three times he headed north to Cincinnati to an area nicknamed Little Appalachia, where so many people from eastern Kentucky had migrated. When he cashed his first paycheck from Ford Motor Company, Hankins swore he was never going back to Kentucky. But in two or three months, when a new mine opened, Hankins trudged home with his tail tucked between his legs. And after a month back underground, it seemed like he had never been away.

"Grandad, do you know anything about vocational schools? Dad thinks I should learn to weld because it's good wages. Mom wants me to enroll in that two-year college over in Cumberland, but I'll have to go back to high school first."

"I heard something about it."

"It opened last year. I reckon it's part of the University of Kentucky down in Lexington. I went to Lexington once to a horse race. Too many people, not enough hills, too much flatland."

"How about the army? A lot of mountain boys join the service."

"I've never thought about it. But if Dad mentions welding one more time, I swear I'll get me a bottle of moonshine from the Johnson boys. They make the best."

"How come you call them boys? All three are in their forties."

"I guess because they never grew up."

"Anyway, I'd leave that moonshine alone. It ain't nothing but a first cousin to kerosene. I only drank it to ease the pain in my joints."

"From what I've heard, your joints must've hurt something fierce."

Ollie knew he could make a go of farming. Two of their three neighbors had indicated they might be willing to part with some acreage. Maybe he could convince his grandad. But how could he explain to everyone the miracle of all those tiny plants when they first peeked out of the ground. Ollie could imagine God looking down and smiling.

Ollie had a deep love of the land and could not figure out why so many families were giving up and selling out to the coal companies. The Adkins and the McKnights sold out last year. Doak Owens said the Hatfields had decided to sell their land, although it was not official. Doak Owens might be slow delivering the mail, but he was seldom wrong when it involved a juicy piece of gossip.

Suddenly, Ollie blurted out, "We can't sell the land because the family cemetery is on the hill, and Little Corey's buried there. He's the only brother I'll ever have. You know he was only three when he died."

"It's not right for a baby to die. It gets the whole world out of order. Did you know Corey should've been named Coy after my brother? But Doc Blevins was hard of hearing. Poor eyesight too. Come to think of it, he wasn't much of a doctor."

A worried look wrinkled Ollie's brow. He suspected his dad of wanting to sell because Will had the land surveyed recently. Will said he just wanted to make sure where the boundaries were. Hankins did not trust a coal company, but he trusted his son.

"Granddad, when I found out about the survey, I was so mad I ran off and spent the night in the woods."

"If you ain't real careful, you'll get carried off by a black bear one of these days."

"The bears are gone because strip mining's run them off."

"Ollie, it don't hurt to have your land surveyed. If you ain't careful, a coal company can end up with land that's been in a family fifty years. It might be yours, but if a coal company say it's theirs, it'll end up belonging to them."

"That was in the old days."

Hankins believed it was still the old days. He remembered that a coworker, Willie Williams, lost his land. Although Hankins had liked Willie, the boy had not been a scholar. And Hankins was puzzled why a mother would give a child only one name. It was not like they ran out of good names. Hankins figured that was why Willie was never right in the head.

Willie had bragged that he hired a good lawyer in Harlan to represent him in his lawsuit. It turned out his lawyer was a cousin to the other side's lawyer, and the judge was part owner of a coal mine in another county. Hankins told Willie he had a better chance of marrying the governor's daughter than he did winning his lawsuit.

Hankins relit his pipe for the fifth time and said, "I see your black eye is about gone. I hear that boy is rough as a cobb."

"He ain't that rough. Everybody said I got the best of him, and he's a year older and ten pounds heavier."

"Doak Owens said he was bragging to some girls at church about giving you that shiner. I could see your black eye when I came out of the outhouse and saw you sitting on the front porch. You better stay away from that boy. He might black both your eyes the next time."

Smoke poured from Ollie's ears. "You wait and see. I'll give him worse the next time."

"Hee, hee, hee," Hanks giggled as he puffed contentedly on his pipe, his eyes alert and bright.

Chapter Four

Hoedown was once a thriving mining town with a population of 8,000 during World War Two. However, the town's population was cut in half during the fifties because of a dramatically reduced demand for coal. Consequently, most of the coal mines closed, and the other mines survived the economic downturn by mechanizing, thus further reducing the workforce.

But by 1960, things started to improve. The despair that hovered over the mining town like a low-lying cloud was swept away as if by a giant hand. The steel mills were blasting away, and cars were selling again. Monumental Mining Resources (MMR), an energy conglomerate, bought Hoedown Mining Company and announced plans for a massive expansion to meet America's energy needs.

Presently, the town had little to offer. Its entire business district was on the mile-long Main Street, where the store owners had boarded up half the buildings' windows. The town still had two restaurants with almost identical menus, two bars with the same jukebox tunes, and beer brands. Hoedown also managed to keep open a gas station, theatre, pool hall, six churches, a funeral parlor, dry cleaners, barbershop, and combination hardware and feed and grain store.

Unfortunately, Hoedown High School, with its spirited 144 students, twenty-nine who still tried to play football, gave up the ghost the month before MMR came to town. If the school had held on for another year, things might have turned out different. But when the school closed, the town that fought for decades to survive hung its head in defeat. Former school board members could not look at each other when they passed on the street. Even when they met at church, they sat as far away from each other as possible.

Nothing was sadder than a small town when its school no longer existed. The football coach, who had two winning seasons in the last ten years, moved to Corbin, one hundred miles away. He started selling insurance and coaching a grade school football team. Even though he doubled his income, folks said he seldom smiled or laughed.

However, a fresh wind started to blow through the steep hills and pumped life back into Hoedown. The first thing Monumental did was hire two dozen idle miners to tear down twenty empty coal camp houses that the miners' kids damaged beyond redemption. At the same time, they hired another two dozen miners who were handy with a hammer, paintbrush, or pipe wrench, to renovate the substandard houses that belonged to the coal company.

Although Main Street was flat as a board, a hill, sixty-five feet high and a hundred yards from Main Street, looked down on the hopeful little town. The entire town became excited when a bulldozer cut a gently sloping road to the top, and workers stripped the hill of the trees and leveled the top of the hill.

For a month, folks walked around Main Street looking up at the hill so much at least a dozen citizens strained their necks, trying to figure out what in the world was happening. Guesses ranged from a new fire tower (actually an excellent location for one) to the coal company needed trees for mining timbers or a new radar installation to detect incoming Russian planes that planned to bomb Hoedown.

Although it was the height of the cold war between the USA and the Soviet Union, no one offered a plausible reason why Hoedown would be a priority target and not the Pentagon, White House, or military base.

But when construction began on a new office complex and warehouse for the coal company, along with a new post office and fire station, almost all of Hoedown boasted, "Exactly what I figured that company was up to."

The flurry of building activity ended a ten-year drought when not even an outhouse was constructed inside city limits. But not everyone was happy about the change. One disgruntled miner, lecturing in the poolhall, said, "The coal companies always looked down on us before. Now they can do it while sitting high on that hill."

From atop the hill, Hoedown might have looked picturesque. But up close, the flaws were obvious. The town had a beaten-down look that rubbed off on its citizens. People often joked that if MMR really cared about Hoedown, they would drop a paint bomb on it.

Three months later, MMR's new mine superintendent, Clive McAlister, was sitting in his new spacious office, facing away from Hoedown, and marveled at the valleys that widened and narrowed without any consideration for the people's needs or comforts.

Former superintendent for Hoedown Mining Company, Bernard Brewbaker, derisively called BB behind his back, when he first arrived in the area, was reputed to have said, "God must have a sense of humor for him to create this place."

However, the county abounded with natural resources. Thousands of acres of rich, high carbon coal, the seams sometimes eight to ten feet high, ran under most of the hills. Also, massive first-generation forests with every kind of tree imaginable, rich fertile soil, high annual rainfall, and varied plant life that would enchant a botanist awaited exploitation.

Five decades earlier, when surveyors first saw the place, they gasped. One man exclaimed, "The Garden of Eden couldn't have been prettier." Yet, challenges existed. Despite one mountain range stretching to 4,144 feet, the valleys, mostly narrow, would widen suddenly as if to lure a company into locating a coal camp right on the spot. Then the valleys would narrow again.

On the mountain, dozens of springs flowed to the surface, the water so cold it hurt the teeth, and provided pure drinking water to the thirsty inhabitants that had ventured there. Unfortunately, the streams fed into a creek that zigzagged back and forth so much it almost reversed directions a time or two.

The company's chief engineer, when he first spied the creek, complained, "That creek is as crooked as a dog's hind leg." Thus the name Crooked Creek came into existence. A few years later, a new coal camp stole the name. Also, the creek's meek appearance was deceiving. In a mostly dry August, the stream would be a trickle. But in April, on at least a dozen occasions in the past five decades, during unrelenting spring rains, the creek almost wiped out the entire coal town.

During flooding, massive, almost perfectly round boulders tumbled down the mountain. When the boulders made their way to the coal camp, they formed a dam and forced the water from its creek bed, and terrorized the mining town.

Clive McAlister was well aware of the pros and cons of the area. But he still thought it the most beautiful place he had ever seen. He loved looking out his big picture window in his office at the valley below. Initially, he was not overjoyed when he was transferred from Pittsburg and briefly considered taking early retirement. But his boss persuaded him to visit the area, look around, and take a month before making up his mind.

The superintendent was aware of the challenges he faced, particularly in dealing with an unpredictable mountain people, an antiquated mining operation, inadequate transportation, and a devilish creek that had to be tamed. He leaped at the challenge. Clive had to admit he had grown bored in his last job, and the promise of a ponderous bonus may have been the deciding factor.

Looking out his office window one day, a parcel of land caught his attention. Down on Main Street, the mountain ridges folded back against each other in a repeating pattern and hid the view. But on the hill, with the trees having shorn their leaves, he gasped when he saw the fertile farmland and rolling hills and acres and acres of massive trees.

The following day, his chief mining engineer and surveyor drove him in his new four-wheel-drive Jeep all over northeast Harlan County to look at land to purchase. The next day, he went back by himself to look at the property for a second time. Someone said it was called Fancy Hollow.

Indeed, he took a fancy to the property and met with his staff to seek advice concerning a new coal preparation plant's best location. However, his engineers, surveyors, construction foreman, and head accountant failed to reach a consensus. Before the meeting ended, he told his staff, "Since it's Friday, I'll wait and make a decision on Monday morning. There will be no further discussion of the subject after I've made my decision. Understood?" All heads bobbed up and down so fast he feared there might be an additional strained neck or two to add to those already in Hoedown.

Meanwhile, Will lounged in a waiting room outside the superintendent's office for thirty minutes. His chair was so comfortable he almost dozed off with a coffee cup in his hand. Will kept removing a letter from his back pocket and rereading it, hoping to find an important detail that he had overlooked. He found none, and that worried him. But if he had found a contradiction, or vague statement open to broad interpretation, that too would have bothered him. Will kept reminding himself that his grandfather had lost his land and died without a penny.

Finally, Clive McAlister's office door opened. Clive was about fifty, stout, and crowned with a thick head of salt and pepper hair that almost made him look distinguished. He reeked with the calm assurance of someone who had once been poor but now believed it could never happen to him again.

"Will, sorry to keep you waiting. I've been on the darn phone for an hour. The folks in Pittsburg are determined to keep me from getting any work done."

"It seems like I've been waiting all my life for someone or something. So what's up?"

"Have a seat, and I'll have Gladys, my secretary, get us a fresh cup of coffee."

So far, Clive had been courteous and was even likable for someone who stood firmly on management's side of the fence. And Will was having a difficult time finding fault with him. Clive was either slicker than a used tractor salesman or a new breed-someone who understood that both parties had to cooperate to succeed.

Will and the superintendent had met three times to discuss the sale of Poser property. But Will still had reservations about trusting a coal company. In the past, management had offered Will a position several times because he knew coal mining so well. Although the extra money had been enticing, Will never considered supervising a crew of men. Will had spent numerous frigid days standing around a fire barrel on a picket line, cussing a coal company until they signed a new contract. Also, Will understood Fancy Hollow was the perfect location for a new coal preparation plant. And he knew Clive knew he knew it.

"Headquarters said the deadline is drawing near for you to decide. We need a shorter haulage route to curb expenses. When the company makes more profits, the miners will earn better wages."

"I've heard that's the way it's supposed to work, but I haven't seen it yet."

"Will, our preparation plant in Fire Creek can't handle any more coal. It's at least six miles to haul coal to the plant. If we can get your land, we'll build a modern prep plant in Flatgap Hollow."

Will smiled. He understood the seam of coal, running from eight to ten feet high, was a gift from God and could be mined more efficiently from the north instead of south. The company had the railroad tracks and conveyor belts anyway. Just reverse the belts, and they were back in business after some minor adjustments.

"What's this I hear about the company building a dam?"

"How did you know?"

"That's what Doak Owens said."

"Is nothing secret here? Look, Will, no reason for Harlan to get the best of everything. Now, young people won't have to leave home to find work. And the state putting the community college in our neck of the woods has changed everything."

"My wife inherited half the land from her old man. By rights, it's still hers."

"In five years, we could have a new high school, new houses, nice restaurants, better roads, even a Holiday Inn."

How could Will learn to trust a coal company after all these years? The companies always claimed they were telling the truth. But truth, like beauty, was in the eye of the beholder. The older miners always said that you could not beat the truth out of that rascal Brewbaker with a sledgehammer.

Another rumor going around was the company had planned to create five hundred jobs immediately, with plans to hire a thousand eventually. But where would the people live? The company had demolished half the camp houses in the fifties. Although Doak Owens tended to exaggerate, no one had ever caught him in an outright lie.

"Will, I just got word from Pittsburg this morning to up the ante to $50,000."

"I don't believe it."

"Coal-fired power plants are being built again. People are scared of this nuclear energy stuff. There's going to be a coal boom, and all of eastern Kentucky will benefit, not just Harlan County."

Will was baffled. As a local union president, he was always preaching that the miners could no longer walk off the job every time management violated the contract. Coworkers had cussed him a time or two for making such a statement. Will had lost his temper more than once and threatened to hit some folks on several occasions. But after he gave the union vice-president a good butt-kicking outside the union hall after an especially heated meeting, the miners tended to give more credence to what he said.

Stop fighting the battles our grandfather's fought. This country is starting to import oil from the middle east. It could backfire on us one day. During Will's career as a union official, he had preached more sermons than Pastor Collins. And Will had preached the same message over and over. He took a deep breath and slowly exhaled. He had made up his mind to sell, but he would have to break the news carefully to Thalia.

Also, this Kennedy guy running for president had seemed like a joke at first. Although Will had disdain for both political parties, this man called JFK looked like he might win. He was even blasting the coal companies for owning mining camps.

A few companies recently announced they would sell their camp houses to their employees at a fair price. US Steel, Bethlehem Steel, the bigger and better companies, were leading the way. Would MMR get on board? He might feel out Doak Owens and get his views on the subject.

Will decided to ask Clive and gauge his reaction. "What's this I hear about MMR selling the camp houses to the miners?"

"Are you a detective, or what? I'll fire whoever leaked this. We haven't finalized any plans."

"Just an educated guess. No need to fire anybody."

"Give me your word that you'll decide about your land in a week. And if you'll keep this between us, I'll give you the lowdown on the houses. Do we need to shake hands?"

"My word is binding."

"The newspapers, television, and magazines are hitting us over the head with this thing all the time. When you say the word coal camp, it leaves a bad taste in people's mouths. We plan to sell the houses for $200 a room. Once the house belongs to a miner, he can shoot out the windows, paint it any color, do whatever he wants. It'll be his lock, stock, and barrel."

"Maybe some bright colors would help this forsaken mining town. No wonder it's so dreary, especially in winter, with all the drab colors."

"As I said, paint the house any color, brick it, cover it with aluminum siding—anything you want."

"Aluminum siding? It'll never catch on. But you management people live mostly in limestone houses, so you don't have that problem."

Clive shook his head in disgust and thought, *here we go again. It never ends.* The look on Clive's face told Will that Clive was easy to anger. Having been a union official for half his mining career, Will had gained a broader perspective of problems in labor-management conflicts. Will understood that all the county's problems were not a coal company's fault. The perception was of a coal company abusing workers. Unfortunately, Will knew that perception was sometimes more real than reality.

Still, he could not wholly cut loose with the past. He thought a lot about the stories passed down from one generation to the next about how a coal company would put a family out of their camp house at two a. m. in February if they stepped out of line. But he had also heard about the striking miners dynamiting the railroad tracks, sneaking in the mines and damaging equipment, and turning over company trucks parked at the mine site during a work stoppage.

He remembered when he was probably twelve, and guards at the company store were tied up, and the miners looted the store. The company claimed the only thing left in the meat department was a roll of sausage. He remembered his dad had laughed and said, "Wonder how I overlooked that roll of sausage?"

Will could remember like it was yesterday when his family only ate meat two or three times a week. And they never had sausage or bacon except for Sunday breakfast, right before church. Will was mystified when they started having sausage every morning for a month.

Will chuckled when he thought about how his two brothers and he got one new pair of boots and shoes a year. But one year, their closet was full of new footwear. The brothers had more than one fistfight over a particular pair of shoes. "I think they were called penny loafers," Will said aloud without grasping what he had done.

"What?" Clive said.

Will could not help but smile, "Oh, nothing, just thinking out loud."

"Will, there's enough blame to go around."

"Yeah, but I'd put ninety percent of the blame at a company's feet."

"According to you, a pancake has only one side. When are we going to move past the blame game? It's easy to fall back into old patterns. Let's concentrate on the houses."

"So, management won't sell the house from under a man?"

"The family living in the house has first choice. If the family needs a bigger house, they can apply for one of the two dozen empties in the camp. Will, a new day has dawned, but it'll take both sides to make it work."

"We'll see," Will replied.

"That's one thing we can agree on. That we'll see," Clive said.

Chapter Five

Thalia, Ollie, and Hankins sat around the kitchen table. They were reluctant to begin eating without Will, although he was an hour late. In recent weeks, Will arrived home late for supper more times than not. Meanwhile, an unlit pipe dangled from Hankins's mouth as he read his Bible, Thalia stared out the window, perhaps pondering Jesse's comments, and Ollie slumped in his chair and eyed his empty plate.

Food sat on the stove, trying to stay warm, as flickering flames from the fireplace painted shadows on the far wall. One shadow looked somewhat like a hangman's noose; the others were a jumble of weird sizes and shapes.

Ollie shoved back from the table and folded his arms. He was hungry. Will was supposedly only going to the post office, but he had been gone most of the day. Ollie feared the truck, the only family transportation other than two horses, may have broken down. Their ten-year-old truck had been sputtering lately, and it was time to get something more dependable.

Doak Owens verified that one of the Johnson boys, Herbert, planned to buy a new truck. Herbert was willing to part with his five-year-old truck at a reasonable price. It even had new tires on the front.

But where did they get all that money? For the last few years, the Johnson boys raised the county's tallest corn with their five acres of fertile bottomland. But they never sold or ate the first ear of corn. All three boys were rail-thin, making some wonder why they never gained weight. They were forever throwing a twenty-five-pound bag of sugar in the bed of their sturdy pickup, but no one suspected them of having a pie-baking contest.

Ollie hoped he could convince his dad to buy another vehicle. The last time his mom and dad left the county, they had one flat going and one coming. But Will was determined not to give up on a tire prematurely. When one of his tires finally gave out, Will took it personally.

"Mom, we need to get you a nice car to drive to town. Ain't that right, Granddad?"

"This road would tear a car to pieces in no time."

"Mom, you'd love a Jeep. It sits up high, and I could drive the truck."

"You can't court a pretty girl in that thing. She'd be afraid the ugly would rub off on her."

"Granddad, I'm serious. Mom, you promised to talk to Dad about it. Don't let him sway you because he don't care about nobody but himself."

"You don't run down your father. Ollie, go fetch some firewood because it'll be cold tonight. I'm getting where I hate to wake up to a cold house."

"I hate getting up before sunlight," Hankins spouted.

"You've earned the right to sleep late. Coal miners usually don't last long after they retire."

"Oh, I'm content with just getting out of bed. But I wished I'd saved my money like Will. But for me and my other boys, Clete and Jasper, we loved to have us a good time. When they were young, those boys couldn't save a nickel, but they could survive on fifty dollars a month."

When the door shoved open, cold air swooshed in, and Will, swaying a little and grinning like a mule chewing a crisp apple, plopped down in a chair. He began to tap the table with his hands hesitantly, like the rhythmically impaired often do when drinking. Will hummed what sounded like a fusion of "Oh, Holy Night" and "I Saw Mommy Kissing Santa Claus." When Thalia glared at him, he stopped humming.

Thalia peered at the food on the stove and said, "Did you eat?"

"Couple of cheeseburgers at Henry's Bar and Grill."

"Those mints you've been eating are no match for the bourbon you've been drinking. Hankins, do me a favor and yell for Ollie to come and eat. He went to get wood for the cookstove and the fireplace."

"Ollie was standing on that hill he cleared two years ago when we sold all those trees to the lumbermill. He's just standing there looking up at the sky. Something is wrong with that boy."

"It's not him that something is wrong with."

Hankins, fearing an uprising interceded. "Ollie lives for being outdoors. He's a walker too. I bet he's walked every inch of this property at one time or another."

Will changed directions quickly, realizing Thalia was angry, and said, "Deacon Cartwright's daddy was a walker. He cracked up that time and walked the mountains for days. Doak Owens said he ended up in Hazard, knocked on some woman's door, and scared her half to death when he yelled, "Mabel, get supper on the table. I'm starving."

Hankins grabbed a chicken leg, waved it like a sword as if his hand was teasing his mouth, daring it to take a bite. Hankins said, "I liked the old man, but that Hawthorne is goofy as a run-over dog. Always using them big words and him not having a clue what they mean."

Suddenly, Will leaped to his feet and strolled to the pantry and searched until he found his favorite bottle of bourbon. He frowned when he saw the bottle was half empty. He grabbed a metal box off the shelf and plodded to his bedroom and slammed the door.

As Hankins reached for another piece of chicken, he thought about his brooding son. There had always been a piece missing from the puzzle where Will was concerned. Hankins raised him the best he knew how, with his mother dying less than a month after him quitting high school. Hankins raised all three sons the same, but each turned out a little different. He wondered where he had failed.

Hankins suspected why Will was angry with him, but he was mystified why Will did not seem content with Thalia. Hankins loved her like the daughter he never had. Thalia once told Hankins the only reason Will married her was to get hold of the eleven acres she inherited from her dad. But there had to be something else.

"Uh, Thalia, I'm thinking about trying to buy back my old camp house."

"That's impossible. The company owns everything. If the good Lord didn't own your soul, they'd own that, too. But we don't want you to leave. Ollie and I need you."

"Don't you worry so much about Ollie. In a way, he reminds me of the men who fought for the union. The harder the times, the stronger the will. The company beat them, tried to starve them, even shot a few, but they just wouldn't quit. I guess when you got nothing to lose, it's easier to have what you think is courage."

"Are you really thinking about leaving?"

How could Hankins explain to Thalia about that Kennedy boy who was running all over West Virginia, blasting the coal companies? Kennedy said the coal companies had made millions off the miners' sweat and blood, but the miners did not own even an outhouse. Hankins was unsure why, but he believed Kennedy meant what he said. Besides, Kennedy was wounded fighting for his country in World War Two, so he knew something about sacrifice.

Hankins remembered all those years that Sarah, his wife, and he paid rent and had nothing to show for it. Sarah was forever shuffling the furniture around, trying to make things a little better. It might have been just a camp house with coal dust sneaking through the cracks of the hollow walls, but she kept it spic and span.

It seemed like yesterday that Sarah was yelling at Clete, Jasper, and Will: "You boys think you'll die in your sleep if you wipe mud off your boots before coming in the house." Sarah had a way of putting things that made them stick in your head.

At least a hundred times, Sarah had said, "When we get our own home, we'll fix it up the way we want. We might paint the outside pink or orange just for pure meanness and to make that hateful superintendent mad." Sarah was forever saying the company must have had ten thousand gallons of white paint stored in their warehouse. But Sarah died in her sleep at age forty, in the camp house painted white all over by order of the superintendent.

If Hankins could get the same camp house, he would fix it the way Sarah really wanted it. The house would have a screened back porch, an open front porch with a swing, shutters, and all kinds of flowers between the porch and sidewalk. Hankins would get Ollie to paint the outside yellow, the trim a medium green, and the shutters a dark green. Sarah was always saying, "When it belongs to the company, it's just a house, but when it belongs to us, it'll be a home."

Hankins fell silent for a long time before speaking. "I guess I'm just a dreamer."

Thalia got up from the table without eating a bite, looked out the window, and said, "There's nothing wrong with dreaming. When a man or woman stops dreaming, it's like a part of them steps outside their body to taunt them."

"Yeah, kind of like a shadow," Hankins said as he relit his pipe. "I'll go look for Ollie," he said and eased out the door.

Chapter Six

The next morning, Thalia got up early, fixed coffee, put on her red and black checkered shirt, cowboy boots, hunting cap, and gloves. Before exiting the cabin, Thalia retrieved her twenty-two-caliber rifle with scope and headed to the barn. It was a chilly forty degrees, and her horse, an eight-year-old mare name Biscuit, needed a workout. They both loved to run in the chilly weather. No matter her mood when she left the cabin, Thalia would return home after an hour's ride, hardly remembering what had been bothering her before. What was it about riding a horse that was so elevating?

Occasionally, she would ride the other horse, Max, a stallion, a bit high-strung and sometimes hard to handle. When she returned Max to the barn and brushed him down, Thalia could swear that Biscuit would be so jealous she would turn her head away when Thalia tried to scratch her neck or give her a piece of peppermint candy.

Today, Thalia decided Biscuit and she would ride over all the twenty-five acres of property—a medium to slow gait. She had even brought a sandwich and thermos of coffee and three apples for Biscuit. There was something important that she needed to see concerning the property.

Around noon, the Posers' truck putt-putted its way up Fancy Hollow into the yard at the bottom of the hill. When Will entered the cabin, he hurried to the pantry door, removed the metal box, and clenched his jaws when a bent lid and damaged lock stared at him. Will heaved the pantry door closed, and something fell off a shelf. He slammed the metal box on the table, gashing the wood, plopped down in his chair, and rested his elbows on the table.

In a few minutes, the sound of booted feet stomping the porch, determined to dislodge mud, announced Ollie's arrival. Ollie opened the door, muttered under his breath when he saw Will, and almost went back outside.

Will shoved a half-eaten sandwich away and barked, "Where in the world have you been?"

"On the west side of the property marking trees. Lots of popular, oak, some cedar. All good for mining timbers. Oak is stronger, popular easier to handle, but we should keep the cedars. It seems a shame to make mine timbers out of cedar. But a coal company don't care."

Will was impressed with Ollie's knowledge of trees. But Ollie acted like they were personal friends. Ollie almost grieved when someone cut down a massive oak. And Lord, he was head-strong. Ollie had recently told the purchasing agent he would not budge a nickel on the mine timbers' price. If Ollie continued to drive a hard bargain, the company might take its business elsewhere. There were plenty of other people who would gladly underbid them. But Will suspected the company gave in because they wanted nothing to interfere with buying Poser land.

However, the metal box, not timbers, was on Will's mind. Will picked up the box and shook it at Ollie. "Did you pick the lock?"

"What are you talking about?"

"There's things in this metal box that I'm not ready to show."

"It's about the land, ain't it? Don't family, land, or memories mean nothing to you? When was the last time you visited little Corey's grave?"

"I just wanted to get an idea of what the land is worth. It doesn't mean I'm going to sell." Will immediately felt guilty. There was a thin line between lying and simply not telling the complete truth. Soon Will would sit down with the entire family and present the facts.

But Ollie would not be impressed with a $100,000 check. Will grumbled that a bunch of dreamers surrounded him. Ollie thought he was another Daniel Boone, and Thalia dreamed of being a famous artist. Even Hankins fantasized about returning to that God-forsaken camp house where he had raised three sons.

What in the world was wrong with mountain people? They prayed for change to come, but then they fought it with the same zeal as when manning a picket line. Will believed folks in Hoedown hated two kinds of people: those that tried to hurt them and those that tried to help them.

Ollie sat down, grabbed Will's half-eaten sandwich, and took a huge bite. "Half the land belongs to Mom. You sell your half, and we'll keep Mom's half."

"It doesn't work that way. Now back to the lock? Did you break it?"

"Why should I say anything? You wouldn't believe me anyway."

How could he get through to his son that he wanted what was best for the family? They could buy a vacant lot in town and build a nice home. Or if they could find five acres somewhere, with farmland and a deep-flowing creek, they could build a brick home. Heck, Ollie was as good as any carpenter around and a decent bricklayer. Even Hankins could drive a ten-penny nail home in two strikes. But what about the family cemetery? There were things they would figure out along the way.

"Ollie, who broke the lock, Hankins or your mother?"

"Are you crazy? Mom wouldn't do it. By the way, why do you call grandad Hankins? You should call him dad."

Will attempted to swallow his anger. Why could he not talk to his son without one of them blowing a fuse? There was something else Will hoped to discuss with Ollie, but it had slipped his grasp. Then he remembered. Will wanted to talk to Ollie again about attending a vocational school. Will preferred that Ollie returned to high school, but he would settle for any type of degree. Welding, diesel mechanics, plumbing, or carpentry. The boy was not dumb; actually, Ollie had a good head but only used it occasionally.

Will wished he could turn back time to his junior year when he quit school a month before the term ended. He had a solid B average and could have done better with a little more effort. What was he thinking? Will had asked himself that question many times over the years. But he knew he had not been thinking at all.

Now, whenever Will broached the subject with Ollie, an argument ensued. Will thought the school had expelled Ollie for fighting. But after talking to the principal, Will got the broader picture. Someone had broken into the principal's office and stole tests in English, math, and science. The math teacher's brother-in-law overheard the two culprits bragging in the pool hall to Ollie that he was "too chicken to go along with them." Ollie punched one kid and shook an angry fist at the other boy.

The brother-in-law, adept at eavesdropping but less effective in conveying an accurate message, implicated Ollie among the culprits. A week later, Ollie and Robbie McAlister, Clive's son, got into a fistfight. The principal suspended Ollie for three days. Although Ollie threw the first punch, Robbie admitted they were both at fault. Also, Ollie refused to reveal the names of the two boys who stole the tests. Instead of being grateful, one of the boys spread it around school that Ollie was nothing but a hothead.

"Ollie, have you thought any more about going to vocational school?" Will said.

"Ain't give it the first thought."

"Ollie, I don't understand you."

"You've never tried to understand me. Not once have you asked me what I want?"

"Well, what do you want?"

"Sell all the timber on the west side of our property. Buy Mom a nice car to drive to town. I'll get a tractor and keep the road graded and graveled so Mom won't be stuck here all winter. The land I clear, I can farm. I know I can make it work."

"You've hardly been out of the county, but you can solve all the world's problems."

"I know my world and know that I want to live in it."

"Why do I even try?"

"Dad, promise me you won't do anything until we have a family meeting. Mom and grandad deserve a chance to speak."

"You have my word on it."

"Is that enough?"

Chapter Seven

Flatgap Baptist Church squatted down between a meandering creek and a rocky hillside above. In the gentle creek, the born again were baptized, except when spring rains made the creek a terror. Beside the creek was a zigzag highway humbled by the unstable hillside above. After several freezing and thawing spells, or heavy rainfall, rocks would break loose and tumble down the hill, occasionally striking a passing automobile.

In the wintertime, cracks in the cliff allowed methane gas to seep into the chilly air from an abandoned underground mine and waft into the sky like a giant puff of breath. But inside the church, on a winter Sunday morning, the children were warm, bored, and sleepy, even though hard wooden pews caused them to squirm so often a mothers' elbow nudged them back to pious behavior.

Near the pulpit, a massive pot-bellied stove, gorged with apple firewood, created a sense of contentment and well-being that even an occasional Jesse Collins fire and brimstone sermon could not dispel. Every time Jesse mentioned hell, flames seemed to leap inside the stove, and the children would look out the windows to see if the cliff had belched gas again.

Also, fewer miners were attending church because the company started scheduling overtime. So when the miners drove to work, they would always keep an eye on the church house and the other eye on the cliff's puff of methane gas. And they drove their trucks a little faster than necessary when rounding the curve below the hillside.

No one in Hoedown could have imagined Jesse Collins becoming a preacher. Not even Jesse. He was not ornery, nor was he a saint. Jesse had loved to drink, dance, and play cards. And he had an eye for the ladies. They seemed drawn to him because he was always laughing and joking and smiling. However, the smile was misleading. He had knocked down much bigger men while the smile remained intact. People often defended Jesse, saying he was not a bully and never started a fight. They simply explained that he was just plain old Jesse.

Jesse's youth had consisted of church three times a week, two revivals a year, one in May and the other in October, and a week of vacation Bible school to boot. That was Jesse's life, but when he turned sixteen, something happened. He learned to drive, learned to drink, and learned way too much about girls.

Jesse's parents, Juanita and Hershel, thought a demon had entered their son. Hershel had only spanked Jesse twice in his life-both times for lying. Hershel had spent many years as a grievance representative for his local union and always complained about Bernard Brewbaker. "He once told me the truth, and I about had a heart attack," Hershel joked.

However, Jesse's mom, a naïve but strict disciplinarian who could wield a switch with the best of them, told Jesse that if he came home again after eleven o'clock, he was going to get it. He did, and he got it. She slammed a belt across the eighteen-year-old Jesse's broad shoulders as hard as she could, and he almost felt pain.

When Juanita finished, she sobbed and said, "Son, it breaks my heart to give you a whipping. But it's for your own good. You're going to church in the morning and going down to the altar. But your dad and I will go with you."

That night, the rough and tumble Jesse laughed until he almost lost his voice. If someone loved him that much, how could he let them down? The next morning, Jesse pleaded illness and did not go down to the altar or even go to church. He stayed in bed. Jesse had not lied about feeling poorly. Indeed, he had juiced down a pint of moonshine the night before. Early Monday morning, he told his parents he was going job hunting. It was not exactly a lie. He joined the army.

While enduring a three-year stint in the army, Jesse excelled at almost everything he touched. He became an excellent marksman with a pistol and a rifle and learned to operate construction equipment. And by accident, Jesse discovered that his lightning-hand speed, quick feet, and country-strong grit and determination made him a natural for boxing. He seldom lost a fight.

But a strange thing began to take place. The more Jesse boxed and inflicted pain, the more he thought about the pain he had inflicted on others outside a boxing ring. He began to read the Bible and joined a Bible-study group, stopped drinking, and started wondering what life had in store for him.

After three years, he was discharged and moved back home to care for his parents. To earn a little money, he started repairing cars, trucks, and farm equipment. He was surprised that he had a knack for it. Then early one day, a lanky, smiling, blacked-hair girl who looked Greek or Italian stopped and asked if he could fix a leaky radiator. The radiator was beyond repair, but Jesse said he could get a new one cheap. On the way to an auto parts store, they passed a burger joint, and Jesse said he was starving. Two hours later, he drove her to Fancy Hollow and promised to return the car that afternoon.

She was in the house when Jesse arrived with her car. A medium-height, burly, and sullen man around Jesse's age was sitting on the porch swing and snarled, "We got us a date."

Jesse removed his loose-fitting, grease-stained work shirt and revealed a rock-hard muscular body that made the man sit up in the swing. "You know a big bully that lives in Oak Creek, name of Roy Baily?"

"What of it?" the man snarled again.

"I knocked him out with one punch. And that was before I boxed in the army."

"Uh, tell her something came up. I, uh, got to get home and see about something," the man said. His car threw gravel all over the yard as he sped down the hollow.

"Where's Lee?" the girl asked when she exited the house carrying two tall glasses of lemonade.

"Uh, sorry, he had better things to do," Jesse told her while reaching for a glass of lemonade. "Thank you very much. I'm thirsty," he added.

A year later, Jesse told the girl he had a chance to buy some land and would work in Cleveland for a few months. Jesse said they would marry a month after he got home. Four months later, Jesse returned from Cleveland with a pile of money. But someone else bought the land for a few hundred dollars more than Jesse had offered. Jesse returned to Cleveland a month later. After Jesse was gone two years, Thalia Thacker got married, not to Lee, but to Will Poser.

After three years, Jesse returned home when his mother died suddenly. He stayed to care for his father, who passed away a year later. Thus Jesse pondered the irony of a three-year stint in the army and then a three-year stint up north.

One Saturday afternoon, Jesse drove to Hoedown and saw the hood raised on a tank of a car, an Oldsmobile Eighty-Eight. A completely baffled older woman asked Jesse if he would find a payphone and call her husband. Instead, Jesse jiggled the positive cable attached to the battery. It was a loose connection. Jesse tightened the cable, and the car fired right up. The lady thanked him repeatedly and asked his name and offered to pay for his assistance. Jesse smiled and said he was glad he could help. Early Monday morning, Jesse received a phone call from the grateful husband who just happened to be Bernard Brewbaker, Hoedown Mining Company's owner. He offered Jesse a job on the spot.

Although Jesse had never considered going underground, he needed something to take his mind off both parents' death. Jesse became a roof bolter, one of the most dangerous and physically demanding jobs in coal mining.

The job required installing safety jacks and timbers to support the roof. A new procedure called roof bolting utilized a rotating drill called a stoper, or "widowmaker," as the miners liked to call it. Workers drilled holes in the roof with the stoper. An expansion device was screwed onto the threaded end of long metal rods called roof bolts and was inserted in the roof and tightened with a hand-held thirty-five-pound air wrench. The work was beyond exhausting.

However, Jesse's mining career ended abruptly after eight years when a rock fell and knocked him to the ground. Fortunately, Jesse fell in a dip on the ground, keeping the full weight of the rock from crushing him. Jesse suffered a severe neck injury and could no longer work. Unfortunately, Jesse had to battle the company for six months before they reached a settlement. When Jesse told the company he planned to hire a bluegrass lawyer from Lexington, they agreed to settle out of court. Two months later, Jesse received a check.

Jesse waited a year before he chose another career. He could no longer deny his calling. Without any formal training, Jesse began to preach. He traveled to all the counties bordering Harlan County to conduct revivals or fill in for a church that lacked a pastor.

One day, Flatgap Baptist Church called out of the blue and offered Jesse a full-time position as pastor. The man who hired Jesse was a scripture-spouting, amen-shouting chairman of the deacons, Hawthorne Cartwright, sometimes derisively called Hee-Haw Hawthorne behind his back. After a year on the job, Jesse understood why someone tagged Hawthorne with the less than flattering nickname.

Flatgap Baptist Church had gone through some bad times in the past. The church's first pastor, Lester Flannery, lasted twenty-two years before telling the congregation one rainy Sunday morning, "I'd rather shovel out an outhouse with a tablespoon than look at you bunch of lukewarmers one more day."

The church's second pastor did not last long. Ned Coltrane served two years before his fiery temper led him to deck Deacon Cartwright with a punch to the righteous man's jaw. The deacon had argued for fifteen minutes in opposition to spending twenty dollars to replace three small window-panes that a neighborhood boy broke while throwing rocks at sparrows.

Hank Groves, the third pastor, was beloved by the congregation. But he struggled financially for four years while driving a ten-year-old car and listening to a nagging wife. Finally, Hank decided he had three options: strangle his wife, leave her, or get another job. Hank chose the latter.

Never one to shy away from hard work, Hank got a job drilling gas and water wells. He ended up owning a ten-acre farm, three coal trucks, and a four-bedroom brick home with a swimming pool. Rumor had it that his wife still nagged, making some wonder if he should have considered his first option a bit longer.

Jesse Collins, the church's fourth pastor, had just completed his eighth year at the church, the same number of years he spent underground. He loved being a pastor most of the time, but sometimes Jesse was exhausted more than when he roof bolted for a double shift. Tonight was one of those times. Jesse could not wait to cut out the lights and lock the doors and go home and stretch out on his couch.

Although Jesse enjoyed Wednesday night Bible study more than any service, he was always tired afterward. And when the weather turned chilly, his neck acted up. Jesse had planned to preach tonight's sermon a dozen times this past year but kept putting it off. Finally, it seemed like the right time. The sermon was one of Jesus many parables, but Jesse twisted it to make it applicable to a growing problem in the church—a disparity between the haves and have nots. Jesse had been a have not for most of his youth, and he never forgot what it felt like.

Jesse concluded the sermon by saying, "One day Jesus was walking with his disciples, and they got to arguing about who was the most important of the whole bunch. Well, this just about made Jesus sick to his stomach. After a while, Jesus told them a story. He said, 'I was cold, and you clothed me, I was hungry, and you fed me, I was thirsty, and you gave me water, I was sick, and you cared for me.' Well, that confused the dickens out of the disciples, and they all starting saying, 'Jesus, when did we do these things for you?' Do you know what Jesus told them? He said, 'When you've done it for others, you've done it for me.' So, I was wondering how many of you folks are helping those who are in serious need?"

Silence hovered in the air, and the only noise was the squirming of small children, the shuffling of men's booted feet, and the urgent sighs of a pricked conscience. During the altar call, one couple who was contemplating divorce vowed to stop taking martial advice from their in-laws. Another church member pledged to cancel a fishing trip to deliver a load of coal to a widowed elderly woman. But Jesse almost lost it when a six-year-old boy short-legged it down to the altar and handed a crumpled dollar bill to the pastor and said, "I was saving it for a toy, but Jesus told me to give it to the poor people." The little boy made his way back up the aisle in his worn-out jeans, faded flannel shirt, and battered boots. His was one of a dozen families where hard times had invaded their homes.

"Excellent sermon tonight, Pastor. Something the congregation certainly needed to hear," Deacon Cartwright said. Jesse had intended the message for people like Hawthorne, although the deacon was unaware of it. Recently, Hawthorne had been bragging about buying a two-year-old Cadillac convertible that registered only 18,000 miles on the odometer.

"Know how I got this baby?" he had asked at least forty people in the church. Before anyone could answer, he always yelped, "The police chief's wife was going through the change and said she froze to death every time she drove it. She threatened to drive the police cruiser if he didn't get her another car. If you drive a ragtop, you got to have a great heater."

Jesse sat down on the first pew and laid his battered Bible down gently. His Bible's spine had cracked, and the pages were in danger of loosening from having been read and reread. Hawthorne held his ten-year-old massive Bible against his chest. It still looked brand new.

"Great crowd for a Wednesday night prayer meeting. Keep it up, and we might get some of our flock back. Unfortunately, I heard the Jones family moved their letter to another church. The church will most certainly miss their tithes."

"We've still got 124 members, and we're averaging about eighty Sunday morning," Jesse replied.

"But we lose a fourth of our members on Sunday night. And last Wednesday, we only had twenty-four."

"I counted twenty-eight."

"I'm the official counter, and I never make a mistake."

Jesse leaned back against the pew. His neck was hurting. People in the church were always coming and going. He had to admit there were folks he wanted to come back, but there were others he wished would move to another state. Indeed, the Jones family was well off, but they stopped giving every time they got mad. Jesse marveled that the people who often boasted about giving complained about an extra log tossed in the stove.

But some families had left the county to find work. He almost cried when Jake and Lucy Shelton moved to Cincinnati when he got a job at a Ford factory. Jake never uttered a harsh word against anyone. On several occasions, when Jake was selling firewood, he dropped off a couple of truckloads for the church and refused payment even though he had not mined coal for six months. Jesse felt there must be a special place in heaven for people like Jake and Lucy Shelton.

Hawthorne tossed his massive Bible on a pew, and it almost flopped onto the hard pine floor. "Pastor, as chairman of the deacons, I've been instructed to discuss our dwindling attendance. If we can keep the church full, you might get that raise we promised you two years ago."

"A lot of people left to find work up north. You can't wait forever for the mines to call you back. My dad, bless his soul, planned to leave the mountains a dozen times. But he'd hear a rumor the mine was opening again. By the time Dad got rehired, he was too old to work. He lasted six months."

"Sad indeed, but what about the Simpkins and the Blevins? They're not going to church anywhere. Some deacons feel you aren't earning your salary because of the declining membership."

"I make eighty-five dollars a week. I couldn't afford to get married if I wanted to."

"Didn't you receive a tidy sum for your injury in that mining accident?"

"Between my medical bills and my lawyer's fees, I didn't get all that much."

"Ah, yes, but speaking of marriage, some of the deacons have expressed concern about your single status."

"Who are these some deacons you keep referring to?"

"I'm not at liberty to divulge that information."

"Well, you can tell these so-called some deacons I'm not getting married just to please Deacon Henshaw. I've done nothing wrong. I haven't put my arm around a woman in two years."

"Now, now, no need for such talk. But some of the womenfolk think you've got a girlfriend stashed somewhere. They say you visit a lady friend in Lexington from time to time."

Jesse breathed deeply. He could not afford to lose his temper again with Deacon Cartwright. But would it do any good to explain that a pastor friend and his wife lived in Lexington, and he went there occasionally to ride horses and visit his friend's church? Although there was a woman, several years older than him, her husband was deceased. But she and Jesse had decided just to be friends. Who could not use a good friend to talk to from time to time?

Jesse knew he should choose his words carefully. Hawthorne possessed a remarkable ability to leave out a key word or change a comma to a period and completely alter the meaning of something.

Jesse fought back a smile and said, "I can't get married just to stop wagging tongues. I've always dreamed of marrying and raising a family, but I don't think it's in the cards for me."

"Well, just think about how it looks to some folks."

"I think about it a lot. But the Lord hasn't told me to marry Deacon Henshaw's sister. She's so loud she could win a hog-calling contest."

"Pastor, there's several things we need to deal with tonight."

Jesse dreaded discussing money issues with Hawthorne because the deacon believed the price of things should not have changed in twenty years. The church had a very reasonable bid for replacing the leaky wooden windows with aluminum windows for twenty dollars per window for $200. The price included storm windows. A church member, a carpenter, volunteered his labor for free.

Half the ladies in the church often complained about the drafty windows. Many said their feet stayed cold from October to March. Jesse told Hawthorne the church did not want a couple that had been married forty years to break up over cold feet. Hawthorne had replied, "I fail to grasp the humor."

Another issue in the church was the poor condition of the songbooks. At least two dozen books had taped spines, and some had loose pages. But Deacon Aubrey Wheeler's brother-in-law came to the rescue. Wheeler's brother-in-law was minister of music at a large church in Louisville that recently purchased new songbooks. They were willing to donate 300 of their old books, many in excellent condition, if someone would pick them up. Deacon Wheeler and Prichard, his nephew, planned to rent a panel truck and retrieve the songbooks at their own expense. Jesse loved the eighty-year-old Wheeler, who limped and coughed because of his coal-dust-damaged lungs but always managed to smile.

Jesse prayed the songbooks contained the type of songs acceptable to an old-fashion Baptist Church. He could not withstand another songbook controversy. The Hopkins' family left the church several years ago because their mother's favorite song was not in the last songbook.

And the Slough's threatened to leave the church when Charley Perceval sang "I Was a Drunkard, But the Lord Saved Me." They were offended because Mrs. Slough's brother was doing time in the Harlan jail for making moonshine.

It suddenly dawned on Jesse that he was dog tired. "Deacon Hawthorne, I'm tired, sleepy, and hungry. Turn out the lights and lock the doors when you leave. Good night."

"But Pastor?"

"Deacon, drive safe."

Chapter Eight

The kitchen windows faced east in the Poser cabin. Thalia loved to rise early, sip her coffee, and watch the sun come alive. There was a difference in the light every morning. Thalia could not find words to express what she felt, and it unleashed a longing in her that could be sated only by leaping on her horse and riding and screaming until both she and the horse were exhausted. Thalia knew she would never do such a thing but feared she was more likely to become a prude by age fifty.

Nevertheless, Thalia was euphoric this morning, from a source she could not pinpoint, nor could she hardly contain. A new beginning every day with the promise of new possibilities and a chance to banish unfulfilled yesterdays. She wished this feeling would last forever. But in a few minutes, it would fade like the morning mist confronted by a relentless sun.

Suppose she could find a way to put on canvas what she felt inside. She had come close many times. But when the brush touched the paint, the feeling vanished. Where did it go? Why did it flee when she was so close? Thalia had always loved to paint, even as a child. And now, at age forty-three, she loved it even more—almost as much as she loved something else that was just as elusive. And she could not quite describe either one.

Years before, Will urged Thalia to paint the coal tipple, the long rambling coal trains, or the burly miners when they escaped from underground with their blackened and grim faces. One Saturday afternoon, when the mine was idle, Will obtained permission from Mr. Brewbaker to take Thalia underground. Will wanted Thalia to see the equipment that cut the coal. But all she could see was the wondrous love of God holding up the roof.

When Thalia was back above ground, she painted horses with manes flowing, running so wild and free in bluegrass pastures it seemed as if they owned the wind. Thalia was afraid if she ever stopped painting, she would look in the mirror one day and see the face of someone she never wanted to see clearly—herself. Thalia understood that fire burned yet lighted a path.

When Thalia stood to refill her coffee mug, Hankins eased his way to the kitchen, yawning, stretching, and limping. "Thalia, honey, did you get any rest?" he asked.

"I fell asleep when my head hit the pillow. But I woke up four or five times. I'm worried about Ollie."

"You worry too much about that boy. By the way, when is his birthday? I want to buy him a new saddle for his horse. He'll be seventeen, won't he?"

"Yeah, August 13th. It's hard to believe. In some ways, he's growing up. But in other ways, he's so immature. Especially with all this fighting."

"He won two of his three fights. I hear he gave a good account of himself in the other one. And that kid was older than Ollie."

It was not just Ollie that concerned Thalia. How could she explain that there was a different feel to the air? That something was creeping toward their family, but Thalia believed it would not happen if she could explain it to someone.

She had pried the lid off the metal box and read the contract. Will toted that darn box under his arm like it contained the secret recipe to the Colonel's fried chicken. But how could she break the news to Ollie before someone else did? If Doak Owens found out, everyone in the county would know all the details.

"Hankins, Will's going to sell the property. He's supposed to meet again with the new superintendent to finalize the contract. I don't want Will telling Ollie first because Ollie won't take it well."

"Better to tell Ollie in daylight. Bad news seems to cut deeper at night. I don't know why, but it always seems worse in the dark. That's why me and Sarah never argued at night. Well, we did once, and she woke me at two in the morning to finish it off. Never good to go to bed mad. Ain't good for a marriage."

"I wouldn't know."

"Sometimes me and Sarah would fight like Grant and Lee, but come nighttime, I'd say I was wrong whether I was or not. Wake up the next morning to the gravy, biscuits, fried apples, and ham. You bend, so the marriage don't break."

"Why didn't you teach that to Will?"

There was much Hankins did not teach his son. Will had been a leaky vessel, and no matter how much Hankins poured into the boy, he was never sure how much leaked out. But Will was not always like that. Will had been a fun-loving, happy kid with a slew of friends. Usually, when Hankins arrived home from the mines, a passel of boys would be playing in their front yard-wrestling, playing touch or tackle football, depending on how the kids felt at the moment, or playing tag. You name it, and they played it.

The Posers' camp house had squatted on a curve on the road. For some reason, the company decided not to squeeze another house in, so the Posers had a yard three times the size of their neighbors' yards, and it attracted kids, mostly boys, like a magnet.

Sarah and Hankins would arrive home after shopping at the company store on a Saturday afternoon, and there might be eight or ten boys playing in the yard. Occasionally, Sarah would grumble, "We'll never have a blade of grass in the yard with every boy in the neighborhood coming here to play."

But Hankins always replied, "Better to have them playing here so we can keep an eye on things. Besides, if the grass did grow, it'd just belong to the coal company like everything else."

One day, a boy whose family moved down the street suggested they play wheelbarrow. The neighborhood boys immediately embraced the new boy and the new game. The boys raced by, crawling on their hands while their teammates carried a foot under each arm.

There were tumbles, collisions, and other mishaps, causing the laughter to erupt and rattle off windows in the Posers' camp house. On a quiet evening, the laughter would echo throughout the entire neighborhood. Boyhood laughter derived from play came from deep down inside and seemed to hang in the air long after the sound faded. *Good memories cannot die,* Hankins told himself.

"Hankins, what happened to change Will? What went wrong?"

"Uh, has Will said any more about the company selling the camp houses? I've been praying the Lord will help me get my house back. Going to fix it like Sarah wanted. You reckon she'll know?"

"Somehow, she'll know."

"First thing, I'll hang pictures on all the walls. That makes a house a home."

"Believe me, she'll know all about it."

Hankins usually lit his pipe right after breakfast. But this morning, memories ignited a fire in him instead of his pipe. How could something that happened so long ago seem like yesterday? Maybe time was not real. Maybe there was no difference between a second and a thousand years. But how could he remember the past with astounding clarity when he could not remember to buy three items at the company store if he failed to write them down?

First, Hankins would hang a picture of Sarah, age sixteen, when they first met. There would be pictures of their wedding and photos of their three boys at every stage of their life. But the most important picture would be Sarah's and his last picture taken together.

They had planned for years to have a professional photographer take their picture, but they repeatedly put it off. Hankins told Sarah she should spend the extra money on the boys. It seemed like the boys raced to see who could wear out shoes the fastest. Clete's feet grew the quickest, Jasper walked on the outstep, and the heels slanted badly in a month. And Will could scuff up a new pair of shoes quicker than any boy in Hoedown.

Finally, they had the picture made. Sarah, in her best dress, dark blue, looked great with her salt and pepper hair. He would always cherish that picture. Sarah died a month later.

This month made twenty-three years since she had left this earth. The pain had faded, but the memories grew sweeter. Hankins could still remember their first date like it was yesterday. Sarah had caught him hook, line, and sinker.

That day, they were sitting on her front porch swing. It was the middle of October, the air was crisp, the hills saturated with color, and the sky a brilliant blue. The day was so pretty it made Hankins sad because he knew what was just around the corner.

Sarah's dad, Herbert Wheeler, was never called Herb because he hated the name, but more so because he wore a size-twenty-two shirt. Herbert told Sarah's brothers, Ogden and Hurley, to sit on the porch and if Hankins so much as put his arm around her shoulder to tell him. Herbert claimed he never started a fight in his life, but he also claimed he never lost one. Hankins was not eager to verify that claim.

After a few minutes, Ogden said if Hankins gave him a nickel, he and Hurley would go behind the barn and not say a word. All Hankins had to his name was a quarter and dime. Ogden promised to bring a nickel right back. Ogden took the dime, ran in the back door, and told Herbert that Hankins was getting fresh with Sarah. The old man barreled to the front porch and heaved Hankins over the banister rail into some roses bushes. Hankins broke no bones, but the bushes scratched him from head to toe.

Finally, Herbert calmed down and had the boys cut Hankins loose. The boys cut the straps off Hankins's best pair of overalls, and Hankins had to tie a short piece of rope around his waist to keep his overalls from dropping to his knees. Hankins laughed every time he recalled that first date. And Sarah would roar with laughter whenever Hankins told her, "I never did get my nickel back from your brother."

Hankins had told the story to Thalia several times, and she never got tired of hearing it. Hankins marveled that as time eased on by, he could hardly remember the bad times. After a while, even most of the bad times had a streak of good in them.

"I'll miss the cabin, but the hardest part will be leaving little Corey's grave. According to that letter that Will won't let out of his sight, the company wants all twenty-five acres."

"I'll miss you and Ollie real bad."

"Maybe things will be better back in town."

"Just keep Ollie out of the pool hall. It seems like he gets in a fight every time he plays a game of pool."

"I'm counting on you to talk to him about school. Even if he doesn't go back to high school, he can get a GED. Then he can enroll in that community college in Cumberland. They say if you do good there, the university in Lexington will take you."

"Wouldn't that be something? A Poser going to college. Wonder what Sarah would think about it?"

"I hear Will getting up. He's supposed to go see Clive McAlister this morning."

Chapter Nine

Clive McAlister sat at his desk, shuffling papers. Clive could not perform any real work without messing with the darn paperwork. Clive wondered whether anyone actually reads the reports. He believed in action, not in words. But the paperwork load increased every year. Sometimes he envied the miners who worked hard for eight hours, then went home to their families and tried to forget about mining coal. He doubted that more than a dozen miners knew he worked eleven-hour shifts.

Clive tossed his ink pen on his desk, stood, stretched, and yawned. He had hoped to make it underground today. MMR had recently purchased a new machine to mine coal. It was called a continuous miner for some silly reason.

Continuous? You better turn off that machine now and then. Besides, he was a stickler for preventative maintenance. Before MRR bought the mine and Clive came aboard, the previous mine owner thought you were babying the equipment if you oiled and greased it.

On three different occasions, Clive had taken over mines and reduced accidents, wildcat strikes, and increased production. On his last job, Clive increased production nine percent more than any of the company's other mines. And only two other mining districts had better production-cost ratios.

How did he do it? During his first month on this job, Clive decided to test the miners' will. He fired a lazy employee that had a terrible absentee record and was suspected of deliberately damaging equipment. The firing outraged the local union president, who threatened to call a work stoppage. Clive immediately agreed to put the man back to work with pay if the president would give the culprit a final warning. Clive understood the importance of the union members thinking they had won.

But Clive had not lost. His strategy was to convince the miners to sit down and resolve their differences with the company without striking. Wildcat strikes often occurred in October, during hunting season. Clive figured if he let the miners take an occasional day off, especially during hunting season, then let them work Saturday to make up the lost time, production would likely increase. Then the miners could tell themselves, "That McAlister ain't half-bad."

Down the road, maybe he could convince them to adopt a better grievance procedure to resolve their disputes. Unfortunately, much of the contract language was contradictory and thus open to a broad interpretation. Although company lawyers rejoiced in creating such a confusing document, the frustrated miners often became angry and vindictive. The lawyers seemed unable to grasp that coal miners were not dumb because they failed to articulate their positions as cleverly as necessary. He remembered one old-timer telling him, "If we could drown all the lawyers, we'd get along a heap better."

Clive remembered one incident when a miner came into the office complaining that his section boss mistreated him. The surly boss contradicted himself repeatedly until the miner finally yelled in frustration, "You'll get yours one day. A tractor tire blows out same as a bicycle tire."

After the miner stormed out of Clive's office, the boss said, "You think he was threatening me?" Fighting hard not to smile, Clive replied, "If your strategy is to lie, you need to start doing a better job. Now get out of here and don't let me see your face the rest of the month." After the boss was back underground, Clive spoke to his filing cabinets, "Sometimes, I love this job."

Clive knew he had his work cut out for him. But he loved a challenge almost as much as he loved a fat paycheck. He peered out his office window, and if he looked to the right, he could see his limestone house sitting high up on Highland Terrace. There was a half-acre of flat land at the bottom of the hill. He wondered if the soil was rich enough to yield a good harvest. Other superintendents had hobbies like golf or poker at the Country Club (management only) or traveled to Lexington for an occasional horse race.

Indeed, Clive had his hobbies. He loved to tinker with his sporty '56 Ford Thunderbird, and he loved gardening. Clive had planted a garden for eleven straight years. When the plants first peaked through the earth, he became giddy as a child attending the circus. But it was more than just a hobby. It provided a barrier between the tremendous responsibility of superintending a mine and having a reasonably normal lifestyle.

A knock on his door right before it opened startled him. "Yes, what is it, Gladys?"

"Mr. Poser is here to see you. Shall I send him in?"

"Please do, Gladys. And would you mind getting us a cup of coffee? And if there's some fresh doughnuts, get those too. Thank you, Gladys."

"Will, it's good to see you again. Have a seat," Clive said as he began sorting through a stack of papers on his desk. He frowned, opened his desk drawer, retrieved a document, quickly scanned it, smiled, and slid it toward Will. "My desk is usually not messy. I believe a messy desk indicates muddled thinking. It's just my philosophy."

"I've known some neat people in my life that was pretty dumb."

Clive roared with laughter as Gladys entered with two mugs of coffee and a tray of cookies but no doughnuts. As Clive gulped coffee, his phone rang. He frowned again. "I said no phone calls until after ten o'clock. What? You're kidding. Well, get Horton up there to look at it. Yes, I said Horton. I don't care if he's hard to work alongside. He's the best troubleshooter on the mountain. Well, write him up, and he can file a grievance. Call me back in thirty minutes if he can't fix it. And get me the equipment manufacturer's phone number, and I'll call him." Clive slammed down his phone.

Will laughed. "Now, I remember why I took early retirement."

Clive had smoke coming out his ears. "Most expensive piece of mining equipment this company has ever purchased, and nobody can get it working properly. If I'm not happy in an hour, somebody will be looking for another job."

Will roared with laughter. Despite his best efforts, he liked Clive McAlister. "Looks like things haven't changed all that much since I cleaned out my locker."

"Will, just between you and me, and I won't repeat anything you say. When you were a union president, the miners seldom went on strike. Mind telling how you did it?"

"You sure you want to know?"

"I don't pretend to have all the answers. But I'd be a fool to think if the miners hate the company, it won't hurt us both."

Although Will was reluctant to trust a coal company official completely, his gut feeling told him Clive McAlister wanted to improve the miners' welfare on and off the job because the company would benefit in the long run. He also understood that the higher the production, the higher management's bonuses.

"How did I do it?" Will said. "I never cared much for fighting. I wasn't like my brothers. They loved the feel of their knuckles against somebody's jaw. But the first thing I did as union president was to fight the biggest loudmouth. We called them outhouse lawyers because they were always talking a bunch of you know what."

Clive squalled with laughter. "I know what you mean. Go on."

"It had to be somebody you could whip-big, burly, a bully. Whip them in the bathhouse in front of everybody. Then act as it bothered you. Even if you whipped the guy easy, you spread the word around that you were lucky to get the best of him and that he was the toughest fight you ever had. Then buy him a beer."

"Will, you're a wise man."

"Another thing, I'd tell the superintendent to give in on something important to the men. I could use that to say, "See what we can accomplish if we use our heads. We'll only strike as a last resort, so we don't lose wages."

"That's good advice."

"Another thing. I remember a friend telling me about a mine where they had a lot of trouble. The company started giving employees their birthday off or let them work it for double pay. The number of strikes went down."

"So, sometimes, it's the little things."

"Clive, it's always the little things."

When the phone rang, Clive picked it up so quickly he almost tossed it across the room. "Is it fixed? Good. And that was the only problem. Yeah, I'll be up there in an hour. Check it over completely. Check the oil levels and grease the equipment. And thank Horton for me. Look, I know he's a jerk, but thank him anyway." Clive gently laid the phone back in its cradle. His grin was broad.

"Another problem solved," Will chuckled.

"It wasn't the equipment, after all. Yesterday, a repairman replaced a faulty breaker at the transformer. But the section boss had the repairman install a used breaker. It was bad, too. That boss will be in my office before the day is over."

Will had read about the new piece of equipment. It was a coal-eating monster. Two giant cutting heads, arms that gather the coal, conveyor belt mounted on the back. It was the machine that put a dozen men out of work.

The men had talked strike, but Will understood the days of blasting coal and having men loading mine cars with shovels was a thing of the past. The mechanization was here to stay. If the industry did not adapt to new technology, coal could lose out to oil. The country was starting to import oil from the middle east. Why, twenty years from now, gas could cost up to fifty cents a gallon, and nobody would be able to do anything about it but grumble.

"Now, on to the business at hand. Will, look over the contract carefully. There's a few changes. We only need nineteen, not twenty-five acres, so the price is $40,000."

"That's quite a drop. What about coal on the property."

"You know it's a small seam-two to three feet high. It runs in and out of the property. Poor quality too. But still marketable. We'll have to move it anyway when we put in a road and level off acreage for a warehouse, miners' bathhouse, and office."

"It's not a great price. So I want a road cut up the hill to the cemetery. You move the cabin up on the hill and move my barn too."

"You're asking a lot. We can't move the barn because it will collapse. We can move your cabin with little trouble, especially with the equipment we're bringing in. We'll set it on your other six acres wherever you want. But the rest of the job is your responsibility."

"Give me a month to move the barn."

"Sure, but I'll have to get permission from Pittsburg to do the other stuff. Do we have a deal?"

"Give me a week before you announce this. I have to tell my family. They won't be happy."

"I'm giving you a lot extra. So I need something in return. We're building a dam at the mouth of the hollow. I want to buy the property in Flatgap Hollow, where that little church sits at the fork in the valley."

"Are you crazy? They'll never sell. Why would you need that property?"

"The dam will sit at the head of the hollow. There shouldn't be a safety problem. But if there's a severe flood like you had a decade ago, better to ere on the side of safety."

"I can't promise you anything. Some of these folks claim their land goes back to the Civil War. They're lying. If they own something for over ten years, to hear them tell it, it goes back five generations."

Clive chuckled and said, "You got a way of putting things. I could've used a man like you. Why didn't you ever go company?"

"Spent too much time on the other side of the fence. And remember, when you're a kid and see bad things done to your people, if you go over to the other side, you'll feel like a traitor until the day you die."

"We still have a lot of healing to do, don't we?"

"It may take another twenty-five years or so, but it'll come."

"Let's make it start right now. But I need your help. I need people like you to help me. I can't do it alone."

"I never thought I'd live to see the day a superintendent talked like you."

"Will, all I ask is that you try. Will, give me a handshake on it."

"I gave my word. That's better than any handshake."

"Will, this is the right thing to do."

"I hope so. God, I hope so."

Chapter Ten

Depositing $40,000 into the family's bank account knocked Will for a loop. He almost skipped along the streets of Hoedown, his feet barely touching the pavement. Will could have jaywalked with his eyes closed, and traffic heading his way would have inexplicably turned down a side street. Along the way, Will even spoke to people he did not like.

Will felt complete inside his favorite bar, listening to a song he had heard a hundred times. But this time, he listened to the music with a new ear. Will could hear the individual instruments separately, yet together. Will marveled at how professional the singers' voices were that he once thought gravelly and stunted.

The barmaid that usually annoyed him with her mock flirting, he realized, had a warm heart oozing with sincerity. So he kindly left a quarter tip after drinking just one beer.

He drove home, hitting a few potholes, but those were ineffective because the ten-year-old shocks had regathered strength and eased the truck back down gently. Every chance he got, Will nipped at the half-full bottle of bourbon that had been hiding under the truck's front seat.

The porch steps that typically complained by squeaking when his wallet was lighter, no matter how featherlike his footsteps, made no sound even when he stomped mud off his boots. He clasped the doorknob and entered a domicile filled with warmth and welcoming spirits into the bosom of a loving family. But before Will closed the door, Thalia barked, "Where in the world have you been all day? After supper, we have to talk."

Few smells could overwhelm the air like fried chicken and linger long after it should have faded. The smell inundated every square inch of the cabin. Thirty minutes later, it was suppertime, almost dark, and the wind had slapped off the few leaves still clinging to the trees. Hankins was taking a nap in his bedroom, Will was snoozing on the couch, and Ollie was piddling in the barn.

Silence yielded to a squeaking door, and Hankins hurried from his bedroom and sniffed and smiled. Fried chicken, green beans, slaw, cornbread, and apple pie awaited the family. A minute later, Ollie galloped through the door as if someone or something was chasing him and said, "I can't believe all this food. What are we celebrating?"

Thalia, Hankins, and Will, who had just slid off the couch, looked at each other, hoping someone would answer the question hovering in the air, forcing the fried chicken smell to retreat.

"My goodness, Ollie. Wash those filthy hands before you eat. Will sit down, Hankins, you say grace." Thalia had taken charge once again.

Will, half-awake, had reverted to a sullen, graceless persona. The euphoria Will experienced before his thirty-minute nap had slithered away. How could the joy of having a lot of money, more money than he ever thought possible, leave him so quickly?

"The food will be cold by the time Hankins says grace. Sorry, but you go on forever," Will snickered.

Thalia wondered why Will referred to his father by his given name. Why not "dad," "father," or even the slightly disrespectful "pop"? Was there some hidden meaning there, beyond a desire to dismiss his father? Thalia had always called her father daddy, and Will thought it childish. But when she said daddy, it shortened the distance from the earth to heaven considerably.

Hankins frowned. "Will, you could find fault with the good Lord. We all should be thankful for something. Thalia, honey, you say grace. The Lord listens more when you pray." Hankins usually remained quiet when Will was in one of his moods, but tonight he felt a reply was necessary.

Will could sense he was slipping down a muddy hillside. He did not want to, but he was sometimes unable to stop himself. "Sorry, Hankins, but you go on forever. You'll even thank the Lord for a full pouch of pipe tobacco." He then chuckled as if he had one-upped Hankins and the Lord.

Ollie had a short fuse, and it was lit quickly. "Good grief, I'll say grace, or the food will be cold before we eat. Why do we have to say grace anyway? A waste of time."

Thalia was livid. "You're not saying grace in that tone of voice. Don't start turning into another Will Poser. One is more than enough."

"Just what do you mean by that remark?" Will demanded.

"Take a month and think on it," Thalia said, the anger barely below the surface threatening to rise. Thalia swallowed her anger and quickly changed directions and prayed softly, lovingly as if she meant every word. "Heavenly Father, we give thanks for your many blessings. Bless this meal and this house and all those who dwell in it. Forgive us our trespasses and teach us to forgive one another and learn to live in peace."

After Thalia finished praying, something soothing and calming drifted into the cabin, perhaps coming through the leaky window. "You sound just like that Jesse Collins preacher. That rascal used to be so wild. But the older women in the church think he can do nothing wrong."

How could a single caustic remark undo all the goodwill that was hovering in the air? Thalia could visualize her swinging a cast-iron skillet against Will's granite head. *Probably dent the skillet,* she said to herself. "People can change. Especially if they've a mind to," Thalia said. She did not want anyone criticizing Jesse Collins unless it was her.

A platter on the table hosted a huge chicken breast hiding among a pile of legs, thighs, and backs, and an occasional wing. One might assume a chicken was born with multiple backs, thighs, and legs to the novice chicken eater. But in her haste to get dinner ready, Thalia failed to cut the massive breast in half.

Unfortunately, Ollie and Will reached for the breast at the same time. And much to Ollie's dismay, Will snatched it and took a large bite before Ollie could return his hand to his plate.

Ollie recovered nicely and said, "Is there another breast?"

A scowling Will, wholly reverting to his old self, said, "How many breasts you figure a chicken has?"

Hankins laughed, "I like wings and legs best. White meat is too dry for me."

"Alright, Hankins, We know you like chicken breasts."

Ollie could not tolerate anyone being less than civil to Hankins. His granddad had his share of faults, but when someone thought you were more adventurous than Daniel Boone, a better puncher than Joe Lewis, and half as smart as Einstein, well, they had to be better than okay. His granddad had been such a positive influence in Ollie's youth; he could not tolerate anyone thinking of Hankins differently than he thought of him.

A long-forgotten memory eased back into Ollie's consciousness. Ollie's friend had invited him and two other boys to spend the night. But at the last minute, the friend's parents felt four boys were one too many. Ollie was crushed when he did not make the cut.

Hankins had listened to Ollie's tale of heartbreak and waited a long time before speaking. "Everyone won't like you all the time. And if you don't like yourself, then you're saying God made a mistake. And God don't no make mistakes. So you just be the best Ollie you can be, and that's more than enough." Funny how wise and kind words from a grandfather can stay with a grandchild forever.

Throughout Ollie's early years, Hankins had taught him how to sharpen a knife, make a slingshot, a bow and arrow, a kite, and ride a horse. On many occasions, Hankins would play Ollie a complete game of checkers, although it took the eight-year-old a full two minutes between moves.

Ollie suddenly erupted, "Why are you rude to Granddad? And why don't you call him dad? What's wrong with you?"

"His name is Hankins."

"See what I mean," Ollie said, his voice growing louder. "You're so hateful the devil couldn't stand to be around you for more than five minutes."

Thalia exploded with laughter. "How much did you drink at Henry's Bar and Grill? Or was it the other one?" Thalia said.

"I'll just not talk at all. How about that?" Will said.

"That would be a gift straight out of heaven."

Suddenly Ollie became thoughtful. "Granddad, I forget to tell you. There's a letter from one of your old buddies, Ike Fleenor."

Hankins dropped his fork, sat up straight, and laid both arms on the table. He looked out the windows—no moon, no stars—they had stayed home tonight, hinting of things to come. Hankins could tolerate the mean cold, the arrogant wind, and the aches in his joints, but he could not bear a lightless night. There had to be some light. If the sky did not provide it during winter nights, then it had to come from a man's soul. The name of Ike Fleener was a lantern lighting memory's path. He would save the letter for another time.

"Ike, Ike Fleenor," Hankins said and smiled. Hankins could not eat. He shoved back from the table, lit his pipe, and let the memories wash all over him. Hankins had not seen his friend from his old mining days since Ike's kids moved him to Akron, Ohio, six years ago.

Ike had more guts than any little man Hankins had ever known, even though he was the puniest guard the company had. Ike even tried to grow a mustache, but it would not cooperate, and the meager whiskers made him look even smaller than his short body and slight frame. People snickered that if Ike had any muscles, he hid them well.

But Ike carried a long pistol, a shotgun, and a lunch bucket big enough to feed four fat men. He must have had a hollow leg because he never got full, the miners joked.

One year, during December, the miners walked off the job proclaiming, "No contract, no work." The miners had given the company a month's extension twice before striking. A few men wanted to stay and work, but no one in their right mind, regardless of their sympathies, was foolish enough to cross the picket line.

By January, the weather turned frigid, and the miners' kids were hungry. Consequently, tempers flared, violence erupted, and hatred seethed. On the picket lines, a short distance off company property, the men stood around the fire barrels sharing misery, a chew of tobacco, or a stale pouch of tobacco for their hand-rolled cigarettes.

February was worse. The miners' kids started sneaking out at night to pick up coal spilled from the railroad cars along the tracks. Ike's job was to guard the railroad tracks and arrest anyone, even children, for picking up even a lump of coal.

But Ike made no arrests. When he entered the guard shack, he turned out the lights. After Ike ate, he left his lunch bucket, usually containing a snack cake, candy bar, apple, orange, and banana in the bucket. Later, when he retrieved the bucket, it would be empty. That always made Ike smile.

The next morning, when the track boss conducted his daily inspection, the boss would comment about the clean tracks. "You must've got chilled and shoveled up the spilled coal." After a while, the company started questioning Ike why he made no arrests. Ike simply replied he never saw any-one steal anything. But how could he? The lights were out. Eventually, the company grew suspicious and fired him. That was Ike Fleenor in a nutshell.

"Hankins, are you not hungry? Are you feeling poorly?"

Before Hankins could answer Thalia, Will, waving a fork in his right hand, said, "Tell us a story about how you were John L. Lewis' right-hand man; if you old-timers spilled as much blood as you claimed, all the mines in Harlan County would've gone union in a month." Will then leaped to his feet, rushed to the pantry, and retrieved another half-empty bottle of bourbon, and guzzled like a man on a mission.

Thalia said, "Will, exactly what heroic deed did you perform?"

Ollie and Thalia loved to hear Hankins recall stories from the past. Sometimes he embellished a tale to make it a bit more interesting. And when Will was a child, he had loved to hear the stories. Now, he detested them.

The strike that year leaped from spring to summer. The miners kept telling themselves if they could just make it to planting time. But a dozen families had given up and sold what they could and gave the rest away and headed up Interstate seventy-five to Cincinnati, Middletown, Dayton, and Detroit.

Unfortunately, only half the families in the camp had yards big enough to plant a garden. Also, the company store had stopped credit, and only a few families had seeds for planting. Although the miners' back rent was piled high, the company was reluctant to kick anyone out of their camp house. Whether the miners won a new contract or not, the company would need every experienced miner they could find when the strike ended.

Hankins detested the mine superintendent because the children were suffering. Also, the superintendent hated a union worse than the devil hated a church revival. But that rascal was born with a green thumb and loved gardening almost as much as he loved firing a man with six hungry children.

The superintendent's garden was a patch of flat land, a hundred feet downhill from his house. The company guards, including Ike, hauled in truckload after truckload of cow manure. Ike had been rehired after a two-week layoff when five guards walked off the job. One of the guards had told the superintendent, "I think we're on the wrong side here."

Everyone in Hoedown remarked about the garden. People said the corn was eight feet high, and the tomatoes looked like red cantaloupes. Hankins figured he would check it out for himself.

Past midnight, one stormy June night, Hankins sneaked into the superintendent's garden toting a gunny sack. Hankins got soaked to the bone, but it did not matter. He loaded his sack down with ears of corn (it was only six feet high, after all), tomatoes, cucumbers, and cabbage. With a little light, Hankins could have dug up some potatoes. Sarah told Hankins before he left that night that she would love a mess of green beans. Of course, in the dark, he would have done a great deal of damage.

Even though it was the superintendent's garden, even a hungry man could not abide the careless destruction of a garden, no matter whose belly it was intended to fill. When Hankins woke the next morning, Sarah was already up and fixing breakfast.

One day, when Hankins went to the post-office-his brother in Akron had promised to mail him twenty dollars-he passed Ike on the sidewalk. Ike stopped and stared a long time before speaking. "Some guards are inspecting everybody's garbage can to make sure everybody's still got a lid. Some of the kids are using the lids for shields when they swordfight. Just thought I'd mention it." That night Hankins buried his trash in the back yard, under the outhouse.

After the second raid, on another rainy night, Hankins got wetter than before. He wore these funny-looking boots that left tracks in the mud, like a tire's tracks in the snow. That night, when Hankins got home, he immediately kicked off his boots. One boot slid under the couch, but the other one laid sideways on the floor.

Around noon an angry fist slammed against the door. Ike and another guard whose last name was Bledsoe (Hankins never cared to learn his first name) said they needed to talk to Hankins. Ike never said much, but the other guard boasted, "I know you're the culprit, and when I prove it, you'll be out on the street in a heartbeat."

Hankins started to say, "You ain't got a thing on me," when he saw the boot lying halfway in the floor for the Lord and all the world to see. Hankins started pondering where he could borrow a truck to haul the family's meager belongings out of the camp house.

When the other guard started questioning Sarah about Hankins's whereabouts the night before, Ike, God bless him, stepped forward and kicked that other boot under the couch and out of sight. For a second, Hankins thought it was an accident, but Ike looked him right in the eye and came close to smiling.

A month later, the company agreed to a new labor contract, and the miners gained better wages, health care, and pensions. The miners had stuck it out and won. After the strike ended, the company got rid of two-thirds of its security guards. However, the company landed a big contract and needed more workers. They thought Ike was too puny for the hard work, but when the superintendent found out he was handy with tools, they hired him anyway. It turned out that Ike was a quick learner, and if you showed him how to fix something once, he remembered it for the rest of his life.

Because Ike had been a company guard, some men wanted to blackball him from the union. Hankins had taken a lead role in the strike and had helped many of the striking miners' families that had a bunch of kids. Consequently, Hankins was encouraged to run for vice-president of the union.

Hankins was elected in a landslide, but he threatened to resign if the local union blackballed Ike. By this time, Hankins had gained a reputation of never backing down from the company in a labor-management dispute. Even the few men who disliked him personally respected his courage and determination. No one cast a negative vote against Ike. It was twenty years before Hankins shared the story. For some reason, Hankins thought that if he kept something quiet, it somehow made it more right.

Hankins scooted back to the table and resumed eating his supper, even though it was cold. Ollie said, "Tell us again about Ike when he was a company guard."

"Yeah, go ahead, Hankins. You've only told the story forty times."

Thalia stared at her husband and said, "Will, have you ever had an unexpressed thought?"

Hankins said, "Lord, I've got so many stories from the past. It's a shame young folks don't know their history. It's a way of life that's gone forever."

"Hankins, the philosopher."

"Will, if you can't hold your liquor, at least hold your tongue."

A brooding, uncomfortable silence had pushed aside the peace and calm that had dwelled among them earlier. As Ollie tore into a huge piece of apple pie, he said, "I've got most of the trees down and cut for timbers. I left the cedar like you wanted. But there's a few walnut and chestnut left. But the chestnut trees look bad."

"Son, you've done a good job. The extra money will come in handy with all the mouths I have to feed."

"Will, shut up for God's sake. What's wrong with you tonight? Are you feeling guilty about something that you've done?"

"You don't know anything. I nearly broke my back, working the mines at night and farming in the day. I became an old man at forty, just for this family."

"You were an old man long before forty."

"What do you mean by that remark?"

Hankins, forever playing the role of peacemaker, said, "There's no need for everybody to get riled. Besides, I got some good news."

Ollie became excited. "Are you finally going to take that fishing trip down to Florida? Is Chester going, too?"

"Better than that. I want to buy my old home place. I've been lying awake at night thinking about that old house.

I know it's not much. But if the company will sell it to me, I'll buy it."

"Granddad, how could you leave this place? We've got the prettiest land anywhere. I'd die before I'd leave it. We'd never sell it, would we, Dad?"

Will snatched up his bottle again, took a large swig, and looked out the windows as if he could see something outside. He started to speak several times but could not get a word out. He took another drink.

Hankins, barely able to contain his excitement, said, "A miner name Tackett was renting the house, but he quit working in the mines. It's been empty for a month. He must've been in a hurry because Doak Owens said he left half his stuff."

Will finally spoke. "Must've had the police or a bill collector chasing after him. When I see Clive this week, I'll ask him about it."

"Why are you going to see him? What business you got with Clive McAlister?"

"Do I have to answer to you?"

"Is it about the trees? I want to get a book on forestry and study up. They say there's a blight that might wipe out all the chestnut trees. Probably all the coaldust in the air."

"Good Lord, Ollie, use your head."

"Our land is good for farming. If I can clear more land, I'll rotate the crops, and every few years or so, let the land rest. It puts nutrition back in the soil. If we just had a few more horses. Horse manure is the best. Ain't that right, Granddad?"

"I've heard that chicken manure was the best because of all the nitrogen in it. Mix it with water, but Lord have mercy, it smells."

"The Johnson boys got a tractor. Maybe we could get a used tractor," Ollie chirped.

"My old man wore out his land," Hankins said. "He thought rotating crops was a waste of time. But our land was up too high, too rocky, not enough sun. Still, my dad never got over losing it."

"I bet a coal company stole it. Your dad should've got an honest lawyer."

Hankins laughed. "You'd find a gold brick at the bottom of an outhouse quicker than you'd find an honest lawyer around here. You just hope and pray your crooked lawyer outhustles their crooked lawyer."

Will finished off his bottle and set it down hard and said, "Your dad was a fool. We went into business with a lawyer and a man who owned a sawmill to strip-mine coal. Five years later, the mine files bankruptcy, and your dad ends up broke. His former business partners bought small farms down in the bluegrass, but your dad died without a penny."

"He was trusting, he was naïve, but he weren't no fool. The Bible says you come into this world with nothing and leave with nothing."

"The meek shall inherit the earth," Will slurred, "but not its mineral rights. Ha."

"Well, the Bible says something else."

"Hankins, don't you know Will is an expert on the Bible, even though he's never read it."

"Know more than I let on."

"Or let on more than you know."

"What does the Bible say?" Ollie inquired.

"Jeremiah 17:11, one of my favorite verses."

Like a partridge that sittith on eggs
and hatcheth them not, so is a man that
getteth riches, and not by right, shall lose

*them in the midst of his days, and at the
end shall be a fool.*

Will picked up his bottle and looked as if he could not believe it was empty. He opened the pantry door and tossed the bottle in the trash, and said, "You're all dreamers. Nothing but a bunch of dreamers. I'm going to bed."

"Dad, when you meet with the superintendent, don't let him talk you down on the price for the next round of timbers."

"Dreamers. Nothing but dreamers," Will repeated and slammed his bedroom door.

Thalia stared a long time at the bedroom door and realized Will was right about one thing. She was a dreamer. But Will had no clue about what Thalia dreamed. She wondered if he even cared.

Chapter Eleven

There were twenty-five heavy boxes of songbooks, twelve per box, and almost all were in perfect condition. Deacon Wheeler could not lift a box, but Prichard, his nephew, young and bearlike and eager, unloaded the rented panel truck in a blink of an eye.

Hawthorne had arrived early, and even though he never touched a box, he stood a safe distance from the labor and freely offered encouragement and advice, but not always in that order. Hawthorne came to meet with the Pastor concerning issues that he deemed vital to the church's interest.

Jesse prayed that Hawthorne had not put on his detective hat and wanted to bring someone up on a charge of what he called "a moral failing." Jesse loved preaching God's Word; he loved the Bible; he loved the heart-rending old-time gospel music that his parents had loved. But Jesse hated seeing a struggling church member trampled by a herd of holier-than-thous. Jesse believed praying for them helped far more than anything.

Today, the songbooks would be inspected page by page before being placed on the back of the pews. The last time, failing to do so caused a mini-crisis in the congregation. A teenager with a gift for art, but lacking discretion, drew a picture of Deacon Cartwright, riding a mule backward and holding on to the animal's tail. Hawthorne, endowed with a wrestler's biceps, was shirtless and wore overalls with patches on the knees. The caption had read, "Hee Haw Hawthorne." Jesse had to visit Hawthorne twice to convince him not to resign his position as chairman of the deacons.

Another of the artist's rendition showed Wally Plummer, the county's stingiest man, dropping three cents in the collection plate. A month later, despite a visit from Jesse and several deacons, Wally moved his letter to a non-denominational church. Wally told Jesse during one visit, "I feel more comfortable at my new church. We ain't sure what we believe, and that's a relief. Besides, I ain't been under no conviction the whole time I've been here."

Today, Jesse was looking forward to physical labor. The temperature was about fifty degrees, clear and dry, and his neck felt much better. This morning eight women from the lady's Bible study class showed up in work clothes, toting casseroles and a cake or two. Jesse feared if the women in the church ever went on strike, he would have to padlock the doors and put up a going out of business sign.

It was easier to imagine Hawthorne without a complaint than to imagine a Baptist lady without a casserole. A joke going around the church told about an elderly church lady, using a cane, struggled up to the pearly gates of heaven and asked St. Peter if there would be casseroles in heaven. St. Peter pondered the issue for a while then replied, "I'm not sure, but I'll check it out."

The elderly lady was not happy. "Well, I might as well check out that other place before I sign up," she said. "But I heard they were having an awful lot of trouble with their ovens over-heating." Jesse loved humor, and at every church service, he tried to insert some levity into a sermon to help teach the lesson. He believed when people laughed, they relaxed and became better listeners.

Meanwhile, half the lady's group removed the old books from the sanctuary while the other four inspected the new songbooks page by page for anything that did not belong there. Jesse would much rather do the songbooks than meet with Hawthorne, who left to get his car washed but promised to return as soon as possible. He wanted to review the songbooks to make sure all the songs were appropriate for a Baptist Church.

Before Jesse entered his office, he stopped to chat with Mildred McKnight, the church's short, petite, energy-infused secretary who just happened to make the best coffee in the county. Mildred worked Tuesdays and Thursdays taking care of the finances, writing letters, making phone calls, and performing many other duties. She was paid a dollar an hour and never charged the church for a full day's work, only billing the church between twelve to fourteen hours a week. She was a gift from God, Jesse had told the deacons on more than one occasion.

Hawthorne parked his Cadillac, long as a freighter, by the front door, although church policy was to leave at least one space for an elderly church member. He was the picture of perfect health, yet he saw no need to walk an extra ten feet. Hawthorne had been a member of Flatgap Baptist Church since its founding, and he believed that entitled him to some consideration, in addition to his seventy years upon God's great earth.

Hawthorne had been a deacon for two decades and always tithed, except when he was dissatisfied with a sermon, which was often the case. He also stopped tithing if he was annoyed by the songs the minister of music pushed down their godly throats or if he opposed an unwarranted program to help folks the pastor deemed needy. Other than that, Hawthorne thought of himself as a relatively open-minded and loyal and faithful financial supporter of the church.

There was no answer when he knocked on an outside door, so he pounded much harder. Finally, he twisted the doorknob, and the door popped open. "Gracious," he exclaimed and headed straight to the secretary's office. "Mildred, dear, somebody left the back door unlocked, and I walked right in. I thought we discussed in detail the need to keep all the doors locked."

"You discussed it in great detail. I listened in great detail. I've had to get up three times and unlock that door with people messing with those dang songbooks. I can't get my work done if I'm going to be a doorman like at a fancy hotel."

"Well, I suppose so. Ah, Mildred, do you have the financial statement I requested?"

Mildred was adroit at multi-tasking. Several stacks of papers always covered her desk. It looked chaotic to an outsider, but to Mildred, it was a workable system. Mildred searched through three piles of important-looking documents before locating a separate sheet of paper and said, "If you'd tell me what you're looking for, I'll be glad to help you."

"That won't be necessary, my dear. I like to go over the financial statements with a fine-tooth comb."

"So you can make sure the ten dollars you gave the church last year was well spent?"

"Mildred, I enjoy humor with the best of them; however, there is a time and a place for levity."

"Who said it was humor?" she replied and returned her full attention to her cluttered desk.

Hawthorne tapped on the pastor's closed office door and entered before waiting for the customary "Come on in." Jesse's office was large, poorly lit, and endowed with two huge leather chairs, a couch long enough to accommodate four hefty adults, and a wall covered with bookshelves. The pastor had plastered the walls with a dozen plaques with scripture. The only thing of any redeeming value other than the plaques was Jesse's beautiful ornate cherry desk and a matching chair that he inherited from his parents.

Although Jesse loved to read books about his faith, he never found the time to read as much as he wanted. He would start a book and then go back to the Bible to make sure it was an accurate quote from the King James version. Pastor Collins was always telling people to read good books by Christian writers but had to remind them occasionally that nothing took the Bible's place. Jesse's favorite saying was, "Those who want to rewrite the Bible need to reread it."

Immediately after Hawthorne plopped down in a chair, Jesse said, "Have a seat." Hathorne frowned and waved the sheet of paper that he clutched in his hand.

"Ah, yes, Pastor. Shall we dispense with the formalities and get to the meat of the problem. There is much to discuss."

Jesse sat up in his chair, placed his forearms on his desk, and breathed deeply for a moment to allow his anger to dissipate. "Deacon Cartwright, that expression, the meat of the problem, suggests there is a problem. There is no problem to resolve. Last year's audit only found a few minor discrepancies and was easily resolved by transferring money to the correct account. The food pantry account and meals for the homebound account got mixed up. It was an honest error."

"This concerns the missing $105 that was never recovered."

Jesse leaned back in his office chair. How many times would he have to explain? That day, he was in his office counseling a couple that had separated but wished to salvage their marriage. Mildred had left her desk and rushed to the pastor's office to tell him that an elderly church member, experiencing chest pains, had been rushed to the hospital.

Mildred had left the money in her top desk drawer. An electrician doing some work for the church had exited the back door and left it ajar while retrieving his toolbox. Someone walked by the church, saw the open door, rummaged through Mildred's desk, and took the money. The electrician saw a teenage boy run out the back door into the woods. They never again saw the teenager or the money.

"Mildred was upset when you questioned her. Mildred thought you suspected her."

"Hogwash. I was simply investigating the matter. Mildred took it the wrong way."

"The wrong way? You came across like a bluegrass lawyer. You asked her the same question forty different ways."

"I am a man of detail. I am thorough in all matters, great and small."

"Have you always talked like this?"

"Whatever do you mean?"

"Uh, never mind. I offered to pay the money out of my pocket. If I remember correctly, the other four deacons were opposed to it. Even your brother-in-law and your first cousin were against it."

"Pastor, I suggested the money be repaid equally by you and Mildred. I felt I was being compassionate by suggesting only $10 be deducted from your paychecks every week."

"Compassionate? She makes a dollar an hour, and you voted against her getting a twenty-five cent an hour raise."

"Budget restraints. Now let us move on to the main reason I'm here."

"That's fine with me," Jesse said, leaping from his chair and saying, "I need a cup of coffee bad. How about you?"

"Gives me the jitters."

After Jesse drank his coffee, Hawthorne began. "We received three estimates for carpeting the sanctuary, restocking the food pantry, and having the power company analyze our energy needs. They claim this fiberglass insulation stuff they're starting to put in attics works wonders-keeps the church cooler in winter, warmer in summer."

"You mean warmer in winter and cooler in summer?"

"That's what I said."

"Never mind. This old church has a lot of needs, but this is a good place to start."

"By the way, as you know, my oldest son's brother-in-law has a discount carpet store, and we failed to solicit a bid from him. He felt slighted."

"Since he had several lawsuits filed against him for breach of contract, I thought it was wise to distance the church from any association until the dispute was resolved."

"Now, who sounds like a bluegrass lawyer?"

After the meeting concluded, Jesse felt like he needed a shower. Hawthorne could make a high-flying kite tumble to earth by spouting his negativism. How could one unhappy person make joy flee an entire room when that individual walked through the door? Jesse knew the reason for Hawthorne's unhappiness, but the Deacon wanted no discussion of his personal life. But Jesse had an antidote for the blues. He was going to see some friends.

Mountain roads in the coalfields often intimidated visitors if they ventured far from the beaten path. Many highways squeezed through steep rock cliffs, and the roads were often pitted with pebbles like pecans in chocolate candy.

The path leading up to Fancy Hollow was worse. The road was little more than a wide path where the trees' branches hung over the road and shook hands in the middle.

Jesse was awed by the massive trees that stood stiffly, as if at attention, during an inspection.

Jesse had promised to give Hankins a ride to Hoedown to sign some papers at MMR's headquarters. For some reason, the new superintendent moved Hankins to the head of the list for purchasing a camp house-actually he would acquire the same house with the big yard, where he raised his family and where his beloved Sarah had passed away in her sleep.

Clive McAlister had even dispatched two carpenters to the house to make a list of necessary repairs. Hankins was beside himself. "Ain't God good?" he told Jesse on Sunday after church.

When Jesse rapped the door, Thalia and Hankins yelled in perfect timing, "Come in, Pastor."

Thalia and Hankins had stacked a dozen boxes filled with Hankins's meager belongings against the wall. Hankins was beaming, and Thalia, although she smiled, her eyes leaked sadness. "Jesse, after I get my house lined out, I'll have you over for supper," Hankins gushed.

"Brother Hankins, I'd be honored. But your cooking is only a half-step ahead of mine, and that ain't saying much."

Thalia brought another heavy box from Hankins's bedroom and stacked it on the pile. Jesse was amazed at her ability to lift heavy objects. "Sit down, Jesse. You're making me nervous like you're about to preach a sermon. I'll get us some apple pie and coffee. I'm hungry."

Jesse could not quite understand it, but Thalia made him smile even when she fussed at him. "Mrs. Poser, if it's not too much trouble."

"If it were any trouble, I wouldn't do it. Hankins, you and Jesse sit down."

Before lighting his pipe, Hankins said, "Thalia's teasing because she picks at the people she likes. If she don't like you, you'll know it."

"I guess Thalia missed my sermon about a woman being submissive."

"I missed your sermon about Proverbs, too."

Suddenly Jesse turned serious. "Which one was that?"

"The one that says even a fool is thought wise when he remains silent."

Jesse squalled and pounded the table with his beefy hands. "Hankins, what are we going to do with Mrs. Poser? She needs to go down to the altar."

After they vanquished their pie and coffee, Hankins said, "Pastor, give me your keys, and I'll back up your truck. Just drink another cup of coffee. We're in no hurry."

Jesse eyed the remaining piece of the pie but knowing he would not eat it, although it was his favorite dessert. By the time Jesse noticed the sound of his loud muffler growing faint, he leaped to his feet and saw his truck bounce out of sight. "What the heck?"

"Sit down, Jesse. Please sit back down."

"Thalia, I shouldn't be here. The plan was for me to take Hankins to the company office for him to sign some papers."

"He agreed I should talk to you alone. About Ollie."

"It doesn't look right for us to be alone."

"Don't you trust yourself?"

"Don't be ridiculous."

"We'll bring my horse into the house if that'll make you feel better."

"Thalia, you're something else."

"Look, Jesse, I mean, Pastor, I've never done anything I'd have to lie about, and I'm not about to start now. Your friendship means too much for me to splatter mud on it. It's about Ollie. Can you help me?"

"What can I do?"

"Ollie said he likes you even if you are a preacher."

When Jesse quit laughing, Thalia added, "I'm worried about him and this obsession with the land. He loves it too much."

"So Will's gone and done it. Has the contract been signed yet?"

"It's now officially the company's land. Maybe it's always been their land, and we just didn't know it. When we built this place years ago and moved out of the coal camp, it took a year before I quit thinking I'd wake up back in that dreary camp house. Maybe we never really own anything in this crazy world."

"What do you mean?"

"The coal companies have taken a million tons of coal out of the ground, but do they still feel the land belongs to the Indians?"

"I doubt that. Some companies have their version of the golden rule. They've got the gold, so they make the rules."

"Jesse, will you talk to Ollie? I believe he might listen to you."

"I've got a family that needs help. I want to take money from the church's benevolence fund, buy some lumber, and make repairs to their house. I hear Ollie is pretty handy with a hammer."

"A born carpenter. I'd love to see him become an architect. He's artistic, not like me, but he can draw up plans for building a house like you wouldn't believe."

"I'll pay Ollie if I have to take money out of my pocket."

"Better not offer pay. Ollie's funny that way. Just tell him it's older folks that need help. That will get him on board. In some ways, he's mean as can be, but he can't stand the thought of older folks having a hard go of it."

"Thalia, what can I do for you? I mean, as your pastor."

"Pray that I make wise decisions. I've never been afraid of much in my life, but right now, I'm downright scared. Something is coming to my door, and I'm afraid to open it."

"I'm glad you said that because I've been feeling the same way, especially late at night. It's scary but alluring at the same time. It's sort of like that canoe trip we took years ago down the Big Sandy River. I know you remember that trip."

How could Thalia forget that day? They had been dating for three months but never resolved the issue of dating others. Maybe Jesse had assumed too much. But when Eli Johnson invited her to the senior prom, Jesse fell apart. Eli and his girlfriend had parted ways, and he just needed a friend.

Thalia had no idea that Jesse felt wronged. He avoided her for a week and refused to talk on the phone. Thalia decided they would have it out one way or the other. So one night, she drove her daddy's car to town to see Jesse.

The Collins rented a two-story duplex in Hoedown that sat on a dead-end street. Thalia found a ladder leaning against a shed in the backyard, placed it against the house, climbed it, and rattled what she thought was Jesse's bedroom window.

Jesse's mother screamed, and Thalia climbed back down the ladder much faster than she ascended. Thalia considered returning the ladder to the shed when she saw something move. Thalia whirled around and screamed. Jesse was standing there in his underwear, clasping a Louisville Slugger.

"Thalia, have you gone mad?" Jesse yelled.

"Yes, I have," Thalia replied. "I'm mad about you. I'm crazy about you. I may even love you. So there."

"Thalia, I didn't know. I swear I didn't know."

"Now, you know. So, big boy, what are you going to do about it?"

Two months after Thalia graduated high school, Jesse rented a canoe for an excursion down the Big Sandy River. It had rained three straight days before their trip, and the water was deep, muddy, and swift. They almost changed their minds, but the no refund signs tacked up everywhere convinced them to continue.

As soon as they untied their canoe, it had a mind of its own. The water was so rapid the trees flew by. Their timing was off because Jesse's paddle strokes were long, and Thalia's were short, and the confused canoe decided to go around and around. The harder Jesse and Thalia paddled, the farther they got from shore. Eventually, they got the hang of it and made it to shore far down the river to a pickup spot to catch a ride back, while workers would load a dozen canoes onto a flatbed trailer.

Thalia and Jesse had a half-hour to kill and to talk about the thrill of canoeing. But once the small talk died down, Thalia turned to Jesse and said, "Jesse, I once told you I thought I loved you. Now, I know I do. So what are you going to do about it?"

The ordinarily shy Jesse, who often struggled for the right words to express his feelings, after a stretch of silence, said, "I plan to marry you, that's what. And we'll have, uh, maybe two boys and two girls. If that's enough."

The way Jesse expressed himself often made her laugh. "Jesse, you have to tell me how you feel about me. Telling me you plan to marry me won't do. You have to ask me to marry you. Does saying the word 'love' scare you?"

Jesse jerked Thalia back to the present when he said, "I remember that trip like it was yesterday. Even though the river was scary, a part of me yearned for the adventure. It was like that river's will was stronger than mine. Now, I feel the same way again. I want to embrace what's coming, yet at the same time, run away as fast as I can."

"Has Deacon Cartwright finally run you crazy?"

"No, but it's not because he ain't tried."

"Jesse, I have a question to ask you."

"Thalia, I don't have all the answers. Sometimes, I hardly know what the questions are."

"You still haven't told the truth about why you left that second time."

"Thalia, this talk won't change anything."

"You said you left because you lost those five acres for us. But there was another reason. There's always been a rumor."

"Don't believe everything Doak Owens says."

"I'll tell you, so you don't have to lie."

"I've got my faults, but I don't lie."

"Except to yourself."

"Alright, Thalia, you tell me what happened."

"A week after the Johnson boys bought the land from old man Spencer, you caught one of the boys, I think it was Harley, and threatened him. He said my daddy loaned them money to buy the land. Harley said he was worried about what you might do. Daddy told him not to fret because he'd smooth things over with you."

"Thalia, I'm going now."

"That night, you went looking for daddy and found him sitting in church. Daddy saw you standing in the rain and peering in the window, and then you up and ran away. Somebody found your rifle outside leaning against the wall. After you left town, the preacher returned the rifle to your parents."

"Why did he hate me?"

"Daddy never hated you. He was afraid of your reputation. Daddy said when he saw your face that night through the church window, he knew he'd made the worst mistake of his life."

"Promise me that we won't talk like this again."

"I'm glad I got it off my chest."

"Now, I want to get something off my chest. Come back to church. You're the best friend I've ever had, and Thalia, that's enough. There's some things in the Bible that are unclear. But thy shall not covet ain't one of them. That's a line I won't cross."

Chapter Twelve

When Will emerged from the miners' dressing area wearing thermal underwear, coveralls, steel-toed boots, and a mining cap, dread snapped at his heels like a mad dog. It was the same feeling he had his first day underground. He felt excitement and apprehension. It had been six years since Will had left the mines.

A week after he qualified for his twenty-year pension, he went into Bernard Brewbaker's office and said, "I'm going to miss this place. I'll miss the men and the battles, but I won't miss the darn work."

The superintendent said, "I won't miss you at all. You've been a thorn in my side ever since I hired you. The two worse mistakes I ever made were hiring you and not firing your dad. Good luck in driving somebody else crazy."

Brewbaker reached out to shake Will's hand but changed his mind and grabbed the phone, and said, "This is the superintendent. Have you got the conveyor belt repaired?"

Clive and Will rode along the tracks in a small rail car driven by Henry Brown, a supervisor who was responsible for maintaining the maze of conveyor belts and for the upkeep of the railroad tracks that ran through the mine tunnel.

Will had expressed a desire to see the new mining machine everyone was raving about, and Clive readily agreed. Clive liked Will and figured if there were problems with the miners, Will might advise him, as long as Will did not feel he was betraying his friends. But Clive sensed that although Will was a leader, he was also a loner.

When they arrived at section five, the boss met them at the tailpiece. The ten-man crew was hard at work. The so-called continuous miner, the size of an army tank, was fitted with a six-foot boom that served as a conveyor belt, moving up and down and left to right. It cut coal with two giant rotating heads and loaded the coal into box-shaped equipment called shuttle cars, long as Hawthorne's Cadillac and two feet wider. The shuttle cars had a steering wheel mounted between two seats facing each other. The driver sat facing the continuous miner when getting loaded and changed seats to head in the opposite direction.

The coal was dumped into a massive metal box called a ratio feeder and loaded onto a conveyor belt, then railroad cars, and transported to the company's antiquated coal preparation plant. There the coal was cleaned, sorted, and shipped to market. Will thought that things had certainly changed since his mining days. He was amazed at the new technology.

After a few minutes, Clive said, "What do you think?"

"Different ballgame now."

"Want to say hello to the men?"

"It's been a long time. I'm ready to go." Will felt sad, but he had no idea why.

Back in his office, Clive and Will were having a cup of coffee when the phone rang. "Excuse me," Clive said. Although the superintendent was courteous, Will believed Clive could be ruthless if anyone opposed him, management, or union.

Although Will was not close to Hankins, he knew his dad had been around the barn a time or two. Hankins had been a union official in the bad old days, as the miners liked to call it. Indeed, Hankins was a survivor.

Even though Hankins tended to embellish his stories and could spout cliches with the best of them, there was always some truth in everything he said. Some of Hankins's favorite sayings were of this ilk: a man who's quick to praise is even quicker to criticize, never tell it all, be leery of a man who's too quiet, never trust a man who's mean to his mother, and if a man's wife can't trust him, why would you? Will thought Hankins should write a book.

The phone call excited Clive. "The second continuous miner will be arriving soon. We plan to purchase a total of five within the next two years."

"How many men will lose their jobs?"

The superintendent leaned back in his chair, hooked his hands behind his head, and looked out the window for a long time. "Fifty men at first. But they'll be back at work once the new prep plant is up and running. After construction is complete, we'll hire one hundred men."

"I don't understand. Why lay the miners off if you're going to turn around and hire more later?"

"We'll eventually process twice as much coal, double the workers in the new plant, plus add two sections immediately. No doubt they'll be some tough decisions to make concerning layoffs. But we have to avoid a strike at all costs. The days of the miners getting mad and walking off the job have to end."

"Why are you telling me all this?"

"Because if you think I've made a mistake, you'll tell me."

"Don't worry about that. But will you take advice?"

"No, not always. The biggest challenge will be eliminating some job classifications. But the man with the most seniority will have a chance to fill most new job openings. But If we need to hire two electricians, we can't have two coal shovelers getting the jobs. We have to use common sense."

"The people in Hoedown hate change worse than God hates sin."

"I love the way you put things. Will, I would be willing to pay you as a consultant."

"If I took a nickel from the company, the miners would somehow find out. They'd never trust me again."

"You just gave me some good advice."

"Anything else? I need a beer and a bottle of bourbon."

"Will, we've got two coal mines now. Eventually, we'll have five. But I want to limit the job bidding."

"The men will demand the right to bid on jobs at all the mines."

"The company wants to limit job-bidding to the mine where a man works. What do you think?"

"You could have a six-month strike."

"How do we avoid that?"

"I'm not sure, but I'm glad I'm retired. Anything else?"

"Have you talked to this Hawthorne character? One of my bosses goes to his church. He said if Hawthorne's not goofy, it's not because he hasn't worked at it."

Will squalled with laughter and said, "I'll talk to him. But I'm not making any promises."

Chapter Thirteen

Dawn beckoned Thalia to rise. The flames had abandoned the fireplace and the kitchen stove, and it would take a while for the coffee to perk. Hankins's absence had already left a hole. Before, when Hankins went to bed early, he would often wake at midnight and bank the fires. Or he might rise at three a.m., hustle to the outhouse and return shivering and toss coal on the fire.

On most mornings, Thalia would gently slide from her bed to avoid waking her husband. She would ease a log in the cookstove or fireplace, and if frost covered the inside windows, both. With Hankins there to drive back the cold like an enemy, sometimes all she had to do was jiggle a poker to get the flames motivated and then add fuel.

Thalia understood that kindness was mostly in the little things. And Hankins loved her like a daughter. When someone loved you without expecting much in return, you tended to take it for granted. Thalia could live without a lovely home, nice car, fancy clothes, rich food, even her mare, Biscuit, but how could anyone live without friendship, without love?

She knew she was not being completely honest with herself. She had love and friendship, but it was like sunlight trying to penetrate a dense forest. It reminded her of when she was a child and looked through a Sears and Roebuck catalog, seeing all the beautiful things—the most beautiful things in the world—being able to touch them but never able to possess them.

When Thalia was a teenager, she had wanted a red sweater and black patent leather shoes. She never got the shoes. When Thalia finally got a red sweater, she refused to wear it or even remove the price tag. It hung in her closet for a decade. When Thalia and Will married and began house-keeping, she misplaced the sweater. To this day, she had no idea what happened to it.

Thalia could see herself walking along the streets in Hoedown, returning to her aunt's house after attending the movie matinee for a quarter. She loped past the department store windows in her tomboyish stride and removed her thick prescription glasses. When Thalia observed her tall, skinny eighth-grader's reflection in the windows, she would tell herself that the reflection was not her. Dusty windows distorted the real her.

Thalia hated being taller than a lot of boys in her class. She even disliked her dark olive skin. Sometimes, her class-mates teased Thalia and said she looked like a gypsy. But Thalia did not mind the intended insult because she thought gypsies were exotic and beautiful.

But there was a cute boy that she liked named Henry Atkins. Henry was the same height, and although he had a sweet smile, he had shifty eyes. He once told Thalia that she looked like a Melungeon. Thalia was a junior in high school before she realized it was an insult.

One day she asked her dad the meaning of the word. He pondered the remark for a long time before mumbling, "Hard to say. They've got dark olive skin, but they don't look like any other people. Some say they're part Irish, Cherokee, and African, but nobody rightly knows. Their womenfolk tend to be beauties. But folks look down on them because they're different." Thalia ended up more confused than ever.

Years later, she ran into Henry at a supermarket in Hoedown, and his eyes were as big as saucers. She had gained weight in all the right places, her hair now long, and her thick prescription glasses tucked away in a dresser drawer. Henry was impressed.

"Ain't your name Thalia?" he asked.

"I think so," she teased.

"I bet you don't remember who I am. My name is Henry."

Thalia started to say I've never seen you before in my life, but she thought that was too long ago. The first cut might be the deepest, but time is a salve if you will only use it. "I remember you. You're Henry Adkins."

He was flattered. "I hope you don't think I'm flirting, but you're gorgeous."

"You are flirting."

"Did you know I had a big crush on you in grade school? But I was timid. I wished I'd done something about it. Are you married?"

"Yes, four years."

"Darn, my luck. I'm divorced. Well, not divorced, just separated, but it'll be over soon."

"I'm sorry to hear that."

"Don't be. My almost ex-wife is the most hateful woman in eastern Kentucky."

"You'll do better next time around."

"My grandpa always said if you make your bed, you got to lay on it. But he never told me the mattress was lumpy and the springs would jab you in the back. But I thank the Lord we never had kids. Did you get any?"

Henry suddenly stopped talking and walked away. Thalia remembered that Henry had been a bit quirky. Apparently, he had not changed all that much. Thalia had wanted to reply that she had children, not kids. She disliked that word. It never did justice to a woman having another living soul coming out of her—always a part of her whether that child was good, bad, or ugly. A man could not possibly grasp that unless he gave birth. Thank God Will never had to give birth, or he would still be screaming.

Thalia thought about the time Ollie, age eleven, had pneumonia, and she sat up with him all night. Will had gone to get Jesse to pray for the child. Besides, Will did not like their regular preacher. Will said their preacher was so loud that folks at the Hoedown Methodist Church, two blocks away, complained about the noise.

By two a.m., Will was in bed, and Jesse fell asleep in a comfortable chair, the Bible in his lap, plopped open in the Book of Ecclesiastes. Thalia gently removed the Bible from Jesse's lap, and chapter nine, verse eleven, leaped out at her:

> *I returned and saw under the sun that*
> *the race was not to the swift, nor the battle*
> *to the strong, nor yet bread to the wise, nor*
> *yet riches to men of understanding, nor yet*
> *favor to men of skill, but time and chance*
> *happenth to them all.*

Thalia sat on the couch, looking at Jesse and then the fireplace. Men. At least Jesse tried to stay awake. But part of what she had read would not leave her. Was that what happened to Will, Ollie, and Jesse? Was it nothing more than time and chance?

Children. Would she ever get over little Corey dying? Again it was called pneumonia, but Doc Blevins said it was a rare strain of flu that inundated the nation and had already taken out thousands of mostly young people.

At the time, Jesse was disabled after his mining accident and was traveling throughout the counties bordering Harlan County and preaching every chance he got. Word was out that Jesse was on fire for the Lord. People all over the county called him to pray for this one or that one.

Thalia wondered why people did not go directly to the Lord. It was not that only Jesse could intercede for them. She remembered Will once complaining that if a miner filed a grievance, it had to go first to his section boss, then the general foreman, and finally to the superintendent. By the time the grievant got a hearing, he had forgotten why he was mad or why the frustrated union members had walked off the job. Was it like that when filing a grievance with God?

Although Will tried hard to comfort Thalia in her pain, it was not his gift. Not by a long shot. Instead, Will worked all the overtime he could stand and purchased a fancy headstone for Corey's grave, foolishly thinking it was the best way to ease Thalia's agony. It only made it worse. When Thalia saw the headstone, beautiful as it was, she almost hit Will. That day something died in her.

Nor did well-meaning people have a clue. They said things like it was God's will for little Corey to die in his sleep, or God just needed another little angel in his heavenly choir, or God's ways are beyond understanding. If it had not been for Jesse Collins, Thalia might never have returned to church.

Day after day, Thalia seldom spoke. She tried, but the words would not come. Even when Thalia held six-year-old Ollie in her lap for a half-hour, she could not utter a sound. Will became alarmed and sought Jesse's help.

"Pastor, she's not getting any better, and it's been over a year. Please talk to her." Jesse repeatedly told Will it was unwise for any pastor to be alone with a single or married woman. But Will remained adamant. "If she harms herself, it'll be partly your fault. You've got to do something."

"I'll go in the morning," Jesse replied. So Jesse Collins put on his preacher's hat and coat and new boots and drove slowly up Fancy Hollow rehearsing what he would say. But Thalia would not answer the door, despite Jesse knocking and bellowing, "Thalia, I'm not leaving until we talk. Thalia, let me in. Please let me talk to you." It went on for thirty minutes.

Finally, Jesse walked around outside the house, hoping to find a cellar entrance, a coal chute, or crawl space under the floor. After Jesse slammed a ladder against a cabin wall and Thalia heard footsteps on the roof, she opened the door and yelled, "You fool, get down here before you fall and break your neck."

Could anyone find the words to ease a mother's pain who had lost a child? Maybe only another mother who endured the same nightmare. Thalia knew there were no magic words to challenge the pain. Maybe there was nothing anyone could do but to say, "I care." Jesse sat for a long time without speaking. Finally, Thalia said, "Jesse, I mean, Pastor, what are you doing here?"

"Thalia, there's no way anyone can know the depth of your hurt. No preacher, no saint, no one—only God can know."

"But why, Jesse, why?"

"Thalia, nothing has made me want to get out of preaching more than seeing bad things happen to good people. Or seeing good things happen to bad people. I don't have an answer to that."

"I'm mad at God. Maybe I don't believe in God anymore."

"Thalia, there's nothing you can say or do to make God stop loving you."

"But why?"

"Don't look for a reason why. There is no why. All I know is that God gives us two choices: we can stay on earth and continue to love Him. Or when something bad happens—and believe me, bad doesn't come from God—He'll take us to heaven to love Him there. Earth is not our home because we're just passing through. That's all I know." Jesse gently laid his Bible down and said, "Thalia, tell me everything that's in your heart."

For an hour, Jesse listened, saying nothing but letting her words enter him and touch his heart, mind, and spirit. Suddenly, Thalia fell silent.

The house was getting cold; Jesse leaped to his feet, fed the fireplace, fixed coffee, and washed the breakfast dishes. Meanwhile, silence battered the windows, and the wind shook the doors. The flames alternated between rising and falling as if unsure of what they were supposed to do.

Thalia struggled to stand, demanding her feet cooperate. She stood near Jesse for a long time before gently easing her arms around him. She wanted to be strong because he was strong.

Jesse grabbed her in a bear-like embrace and began to cry softly. Gradually, his cries turned to anguish, his entire body shaking-gut-wrenching sobs that came from deep inside him. She had never seen such sorrow come from another human being. Jesse cried and cried.

Finally, Thalia found her voice, still cracking and wavering and fighting for enough strength to utter, "It's, it's okay, Jesse. It's going to be alright. Don't cry, Jesse. Please don't cry. It's going to be alright. It's going to get better."

Jesse stopped sobbing but continued to cry softly. Thalia clasped Jesse in a powerful hug and whispered, "I know it's going to be alright."

Suddenly, the sunlight lifted the burden. The sun, humbled all day, shoved back the gray and was now dominating the sky. The sky was a dazzling blue that had to be the color of heaven. Thalia had known the love of family, friends, and the love of life itself. But now, she felt love like she had never known. She had never felt the presence of God so strongly in her life.

The cabin was aglow with a spirit of something so good, so pure, so beautiful, that she had no words for it. Although Thalia had read John 3:16 more times than she could count, the message had never been more clear, more powerful, more true: "For God so loved the world that he gave His only begotten Son..." she was unable to finish it. It was too much. She could barely contain herself.

"Jesse, your coffee is strong enough to float a steel-toed boot. Sit down, and I'll fix us a fresh pot. Do you like apple pie? Will says I would win first place at the county fair. But I'll let you be the judge."

"Thalia, I'm so sorry. I'm a poor excuse for a pastor, falling apart on you like that. Forgive me for not being strong for you."

"Jesse Collins, you have no idea how strong you are."

"I don't know what I've done."

"Jesse, you're right. You have no idea what you've done."

Thalia was jarred back into reality when the sound of a bedroom door creaked, and a voice said, "Mom, mind fixing me some breakfast? I've got to get going this morning. I hired the sawmill to haul the timbers over to the coal company. They get a third of the timbers for us using their trucks."

"Sounds fair to me," Thalia replied. "Sit down, honey, and I'll get your coffee." The fire was blazing, the sun was shining, and a feeling of contentment swarmed Thalia. She knew it would be a good day to paint something.

Chapter Fourteen

Hankins could not believe it. The house now belonged to him. He paid $800 to purchase a four-room home and a coal house to boot. Later, the outhouse could become a tool shed.

Company carpenters had installed a small bathroom with a standup shower, toilet, and washbasin. Workers patched the plastered walls and ceiling and painted the entire inside of the house beige. Workers also installed new electrical wiring and tripled the clothes closet's size in the two bedrooms. The front porch floor was dilapidated, so the carpenters nailed down the four-inch-wide tongue and groove flooring. The repair bill totaled $100, payable ten dollars monthly. Hankins thought he had died and gone to heaven. The bill had to be a mistake.

Although the outside of the house and the coal house begged for paint, the carpenters said Hankins would be responsible for those repairs. Hankins could not climb a ladder because he was too unsteady on his feet. But Ollie would take over the repairs.

Hankins still had two dozen boxes stacked in the corner. But he would wait on Ollie for that, too. Hankins's philosophy was to keep a boy busy, and that would keep him out of jail. It had worked with all three of his boys. He just wished Clete and Jasper would move back home, or at least visit more often. Will could use his brothers around him. But Clete and Jasper had left Harlan County as soon as possible. They both had believed something grand and exciting awaited them elsewhere.

Clete graduated a year before Jasper but promised to wait until his brother was out of school, so they could head north. But a week after Clete graduated, Jasper, a junior, said, "I don't see no need for more schooling. I'm ready to make me some money." The next day they left for Middletown, Ohio, where many people had moved from eastern Kentucky. They both got jobs in a steel mill and never missed a day of work, other than vacation, for the first three years. Unfortunately, they only came home twice a year to visit family.

Hankins missed his fun-loving sons. Whether they were hunting, fishing, playing horseshoes, or singing Hank Williams's songs at family gatherings, they thought where they were was the place to be. Strangers flocked to them like rabbits to a carrot patch. Their unbridled joy for living rubbed off on everyone who happened to pass by.

The only drawback to Cleve and Jasper was their relationship with the opposite sex. They both liked women, but neither could figure out how to stay married. Clete hated the single life and felt that he had lost something he could never regain—affection, companionship, trust.

Divorce to Jasper was like being paroled from a martial prison and regaining what he thought was freedom by disposing of his obligation to another person. Neither one had fathered children, but Hankins prayed it would happen one day. He needed more than one grandchild to love.

Clete and Jasper were cut from the same bolt of cloth. Both were crazy about gravy and biscuits, fried chicken and pinto beans and cornbread. Both refused to own any vehicle but a Ford truck.

But they had their differences. Clete loved the Lord, and Jasper, despite his upbringing, ran away from the church as fast as he could. He might knock down a scoffer with the same enthusiasm as he would someone who opposed a union, but he would cuss when Clete invited him to church.

There were other differences. Cleve married the first girl he dated. Although Clete had been a faithful and doting husband, his wife started cheating six months after being married. Incredibly, she said everything was his fault. And no matter what he did, she criticized him. If he worked overtime, she said he was a poor manager with money. If he turned down the overtime, she said he was too lazy to work. They had split up four times in three years, and Clete finally had enough. Yet, she still occasionally asked him for money despite being divorced for fifteen years. Recently, when she got her third car repossessed, she asked Clete to help get it back.

Over the years, Clete seldom dated, but he rediscovered his first love. After being lonely, listless, and lost for several years, his faith came roaring back to life. He became devout once again and regained the joy of his salvation. At forty-eight, he was a dedicated Sunday school teacher and supported his church in labor and finances. He was content.

But folks repeatedly tried to fix him up. They would say something like, "Clete, my sister's husband ran off, and he's been gone eight years. The court declared him legally dead. I think you two would get along great." Or they would say, "Ain't you tired of being alone?" Clete always replied, "You ain't never alone when you got Jesus."

Now that he no longer cared about a relationship, he could not attend a church function without a half-dozen women surrounding him like flies around a glass of buttermilk. Could a woman sense when a man was hurting and needy? Maybe a man gave off vibes that made his head of thick wavy hair, bulging muscles, and a perfectly shaped face mean nothing. It seemed like when an insecure man asked a woman to dance, she would escape from his presence like someone fleeing a house fire.

And if that same man decided romance was not high on his list, a woman would drive ten miles out of her way to accidentally bump into him at a grocery store. Or walk past five empty church pews and squeeze into an overcrowded row and say, "Is this seat taken?" It was a mystery he would never be able to solve.

However, flip the pancake over, and the opposite was true with Jasper. All three of his wives had been faithful, forgiving, and fun. His first wife was tall, lovely, and thin, the second one was short, round, and cute, and the third one was plain and straw-headed but filled a pair of tight denim jeans that would knock a drunk off a barstool in any honky-tonk in Harlan County.

The brothers got together every Saturday morning and ate a hearty breakfast at a family restaurant because it reminded Jasper of a place back in Kentucky. Jasper liked Middletown but always said, "It's almost home, but it ain't home. Clete, if I die before you, bury me back in hills where I belong."

Clete always replied, "I'll take you back home if it ain't too much trouble."

Jasper would bellow, "You better do it."

"If I don't, what will you do about it?"

Although Jasper never re-married, he could not stand to be alone for an extended period. He would settle down with a woman for about a year, and then he would start nit-picking. It always started with him faulting the gravy. It was either too thin, too thick, or too lumpy.

If a woman broached the subject of a permanent relationship, Jasper would dump her quicker than he would hand a torn fifty-dollar bill back to a store clerk.

If his girlfriend bought a new bedspread or tablecloth for his house, he would give her a month to get gone. "A woman starts doing such, she's done figured out she's got you hooked. A man has to be careful these days," Jasper said. "If you come home from work and she's moved the couch, that's another red flag."

But Jasper saved the best for last. He said if he liked a woman, he could go up to two years, but that was the limit. After her time was up, Jasper would say, "I pay alimony to three ex-wives, and I ain't got a penny saved. They even laid a claim to my pension and social security."

"Jasper, have no shame?" Clete often said.

"If they're still around, I'd keep on. I'd say there's two mortgages on the house, and it's still in my second wife's name. Lord, I should've got me a good lawyer."

"You need to get back in church quick."

"Clete, if they ain't fainted by then, I'd give it some more. I'd say can you borrow about three grand for me to catch up? Usually, in a day or two, they'd have their bags packed and ready to go."

"Jasper, if you had a good woman, you'd just kick her out the first time she burned the biscuits."

Jasper became angry and said, "You're a fine one to give advice. You got your heart broke more with that one woman than with me rooting for the Cincinnati Reds all these years. Brother, take my advice and don't ever let a woman from Harlan County move in. It'll take a trainload of gun thugs to get her out."

"Come to church and find you a good woman."

"If that's the case, why ain't you latched on to one?"

"Because I'm like Dad. One woman for one man. The way God intended it."

"Clete, I swear, you wear me out just talking to you. Say, brother, let's go home for Christmas this year. I miss the old man something awful. I almost wrote him a letter last week. Do you still write Dad?"

"Every month. If Dad gets a phone now that he's back in town, we can call him every week. Jasper, our dad won't be around forever."

"I know; I just don't like to think about it."

"Jasper, we need to go see Will, too."

"Yeah, I know. The blockhead. If I could find me a woman like that Thalia, I get married in a week."

"It wouldn't last long. If the woman was like Thalia, you'd be dead in three days."

"Hee, hee, hee. Ain't that the truth."

Hankins stopped reminiscing long enough to relight his pipe. He eased back and forth in his new rocking chair and let the memories wash him clean. What in the world had he done wrong? Clete was afraid to take another chance, even with a churchwoman. Jasper, for all his bravado, feared to let someone see the real him. And Will could not grasp that he made women sad.

Hankins prayed that one day he would have another grandchild to hold in his lap and tell them stories. He hoped before he passed from this life, he would have a sweet little granddaughter to spoil. Hankins almost dozed off when he heard footsteps on the porch and then a loud knock. Ollie lumbered into the front room and said, "Hey, somebody's been painting."

"The whole house," Hankins beamed.

"You're kidding. The company even patched the plaster. You must've knowed something bad about somebody. A coal company don't do stuff like that."

"Just lucky, I guess."

"Granddad, I'll wait until spring to paint the outside of the house. But I'll get up on the roof today and check out the shingles and the chimney. These old chimneys get in bad shape over the years. Cracks, creosote buildup from burning pine. I'll bring you a truckload or two of oak before too long."

"I'll pay you."

"No, you won't. Just fix me some coffee whenever I come over. I'm getting paid for cutting timbers, so I'll make plenty of money. The company usually wants six-footers. But they've hit a bigger seam of coal and need mostly seven and eight footers. More work but more money."

"You need anything?"

"Going to buy me a good used pickup. Herbert Johnson wants to sell his. New front tires."

"Those boys have sold so much moonshine they'll probably buy themselves a bluegrass farm and breed racehorses."

"They ain't got enough sense to even plant a garden. All the Johnson boys know is making moonshine, racing cars, and chasing girls."

"Nothing wrong with that last thing. I hear those boys like to fight. How old are they now? I'd guess forty-one, forty-two, and forty-three. Their old man was consistent."

"They do like to fight. But only if it's somebody that can't or won't fight back."

"Ollie, you stay away from those boys."

"They ain't as bad as people think."

"They're bad enough. By the way, Feel like lifting all these boxes?"

"That's why I'm here, Granddad. That's why I'm here."

Chapter Fifteen

Will's truck bumped along Poser property on dirt-packed and narrow paths, with tree limbs and bushes grabbing at both sides of the vehicle. In decades past, the forestry service had cut fire breaks throughout the twenty-five acres, but nature had regained the upper hand, and most of the roads were impassable.

Will stopped the truck on top of a hill and looked down below. Ollie was sitting under a tree, surrounded by three gasoline chain saws, two five-gallon gas cans, and a big metal lunch pail.

Will started walking the hundred yards down the hill to get a good look at the land. He was determined to talk to Ollie about the sale. Even though Ollie was sitting on what was now company property, the contract stated Ollie could cut trees on MMR's nineteen acres for another year.

Will wondered how Ollie got down there with all his equipment? Then he saw Ollie's horse staked behind a gathering of trees, casually nibbling what little grass remained. The company was raring to clear the trees and level the land and would not hesitate to bulldoze chestnut, walnut, beech, maple, or cherry. It was hard for Will to understand that beautiful hardwood trees held no value to a coal company other than for timbers.

He decided he would let Thalia talk to Ollie first. She had a calming effect on the boy, whereas he made Ollie angry every time they spoke. Thalia was always saying, "Put your arm around his shoulder or hug him and tell him that you love him."

"That would embarrass the boy," Will always replied.

"Who cares? When Ollie's grown up, that day will mean a lot more than it does now." Will had planned on hugging Ollie many times, but he just never got around to it. Right now, he needed a beer or two and wanted to get out of town.

Crooked Creek was a town three times the size of Hoedown. The community always had bigger and more modern coal mines and could withstand a much bigger downturn in the market than the smaller companies around Hoedown.

An energy conglomerate that owned Angel Coal Company had invested in coal, oil, gas, and even timber. Clive said for a company to survive, it had to diversify. But Angel Coal Company had another advantage. Their coal was a high-carbon, high-BTU, low-ash grade sold at a higher price, mostly to the steel mills that tended to shun the lower-grade coal. Will wondered if Angel Coal Company's coal ended up in the steel mill in Middletown, Ohio, where his brothers worked. He would have to find out.

Anyway, the bars in Crooked Creek, particularly the Rooster's Coop, were much nicer than Hoedown's bars. But on the way to Crooked Creek, Will stopped at the first bar he passed. He took a shortcut down three miles of gravel road that zig-zagged the entire way. The careless bulldozer operator may have been hitting the moonshine the night before because if the road were a little straighter, it would have eliminated a half-mile distance to a paved road.

Up ahead, Will spied Ed's Place. It was a dump. The bar's small parking lot was always muddy because a tiny stream trickled down a hill except during August. A few wheelbarrows of gravel had been scattered on the parking lot, but mud still held the upper hand. At most, the lot could handle eight vehicles if parked sensibly, but that seldom happened with a bar's patrons.

Fortunately, there was only one car and one truck on the lot at six p.m. It had been two years since Will last visited the place. The bar was little more than a two-room shack with six rickety booths, an antique cooler for beer, wine, soda, a jukebox, a pinball machine, and a pool table. At the bar's entrance, a beer sign above the door buzzed politely and blinked, perhaps trying to decide if it wanted to keep working or not. A clock behind the bar announced five before nine, but the clock had given up the ghost long ago.

Years ago, Will and his brothers had loved to play the pinball machine. Will was slow with the flippers, Clete too fast, but Jasper was a wizard. A contestant played the game with five steel balls. To win a game required getting at least three balls in a roll, across, or down. Four balls in a roll won a dollar; five in a roll netted a player five dollars.

Gloom hung heavy in the bar. A beefy, unshaven, scowling bartender leaned on a rickety plywood bar that was warped and splintered and sagged under his weight. On a wall behind the counter was a rack holding a dozen dusty bags of chips of a wide variety. Will, who disliked clutter and a messy house, even though he seldom helped to make it otherwise, fought an urge to grab the bartender's soiled rag and wipe the bags clean.

The bar was once comfortably run-down but now was battered by neglect. The ceiling was a smoke-stained yellow, its glory days of white long gone. The floor was unpainted warped plywood, and cigarette butts littered the floor, and scuffed boots had kicked at the splinters. If Will remembered correctly, the jukebox was full of tunes about broken hearts, still two for a quarter.

A toilet hid in a back closet that had never met bleach. It was worse than a neglected outhouse. At least in an outhouse, you could scatter a handful of lime and reduce the burden of necessity.

Ed's Place reminded him of a bar back in Hoedown that burned down a decade ago. He had hurried there every time Thalia and he had quarreled. Will had often looked for an excuse to get out of the house so he could dream about a better or different way of life. A life away from the brute labor, methane gas, and unstable roof of a coal mine.

The first five years of their marriage, Will tried to convince Thalia for them to leave Kentucky and join his brothers in Middletown, but she would not budge. "Thalia, you get along better with Clete and Jasper than you do with me. What have you got to lose?" Will would say.

"Nothing but my roots, my church, and land that's been in the family forty years. That's all."

Part of the problem was that two of her brothers, George, killed in action in the Korean War, and Troy, electrocuted in a mining accident, was buried on Hoedown's other side, near Jesse Collins's property. She felt it was her duty to care for the graves.

Thalia's two remaining brothers, Milton, was hunkered down in Detroit, and Truman, in what seemed like a foreign country, was stuck in California. Truman had not been home in six years, and Milton had not visited in two years, although they both wrote Thalia occasionally. Her brothers, after all these years, still thought Thalia could do no wrong. If they lived nearby and thought she was unhappy, they would investigate.

Thalia said she would never give up the eleven acres her dad left her. She repeatedly told Will, "You can go, but I'm staying on daddy's land." What in the world was wrong with her? Still calling him daddy. Creative people were a different breed. People who liked writing, painting, or music, often lived in a world where realistic and practical people could seldom feel at home.

In the past, after Will imbibed an abundance of brew, he would stare at Thalia while she concentrated intently on a drawing or painting. In those rare moments, Will thought he caught a glimpse of the real her. But if the wind rattled a window or door, or if flickering flames in the fireplace caught his attention or a dozen other things interrupted the flow, the insight vanished as quickly as it came. She once said, "Would you like to take a look at what I'm doing?" He often replied, "Uh, not now, maybe later." It had been a decade since Thalia had offered to let him see any of her work.

But Will was a realist, not a dreamer. Oh, he could appreciate the beauty of a sunrise, sunset, or a hundred red-bud trees overtaking the hills in April, or the green-black color of the foliage in midsummer. But did that mean he had to become goofy and drift off into another world?

Two customers sat at one of the six booths farthest from the door. Although the bar sold beer and wine only, a fifth of bourbon rested on their table. Neither of the men took a drink, perhaps waiting on the other to tilt the half-empty bottle upwards. The younger of the two men, about thirty and a head shorter, was consoling his friend. He placed his hand on the older man's lumberjack shoulders and said, "Dan, you should've talked to her first husband before you got hitched."

"I added a room on the house just to please her, and it already had a thousand square feet."

"Some women want it all. Dan, she was always unhappy about something. It seemed like she threatened to leave every Saturday, except payday weekend."

"Gary, I lay awake at night, thinking I'll hear her come in the front door. I've been leaving the door unlocked."

"Good Lord. The Johnson boys only live down the road two or three miles. They'd steal the hat off your head if they thought they'd get a quarter for it. They do make good moonshine, but the rascals have raised their prices this year."

Dan said nothing as he stared at the bottle, waiting for Gary to grab it. Finally, Dan clasped the bottle with hands that looked as if they could bend a steel bar. His granite face rested atop a bulging neck. He reeked with power as he slid from the booth and eased across the floor to the jukebox. He stood for a long time before dropping in several coins, and the saddest song Will ever heard began to play:

> *Some folks live just for takin'*
> *And some live just for givin'*
> *But you ain't really livin'*
> *If you ain't never lovin'.*

Will decided one beer tonight was enough. He was going home and talk to his wife. He certainly did not want to trade places with Dan or even Gary. Maybe hanging out in Ed's Place was fine when you were twenty, but not thirty or forty. It was such a slow process; you had no way of knowing you had embraced defeat until it was too late. As Will exited the bar, the beer sign above the door buzzed goodnight and then went dark.

Chapter Sixteen

When quiet finally tiptoed from the corners of the cabin, Thalia arose from napping on the couch. She light-footed it to the kitchen and smiled when the clock said it was a little past six p.m. Thalia hoped to have an hour's silence, a buffer between her secret thoughts and life's challenges before Will came home. Fortunately, he was late again.

The kitchen was warm. It would take little effort for a roaring fire to evict the cold and to perk some coffee. Ollie had added firewood to the coal stove and fireplace a short time earlier before taking off on his horse. She had meant to talk to him, but she fell asleep.

Thalia wondered after the company moved the cabin if it would still feel like home. Will had briefly considered buying a camp house in Hoedown, but Thalia talked him out of it. "We'd be lucky to get Ollie to spend one night in the place," she said. Will grumbled but finally agreed with Thalia. Ollie had said more than once that hell was probably a coal camp with uglier camp houses and smaller yards than Hoedown.

The company had changed its initial location for a road, and now the Posers' cabin would not be in the way. The superintendent said the cabin would likely be relocated in May. The cabin would rest on a hill below Little Corey's grave overlooking the valley and reduce the two miles to town to a half-mile.

By springtime, electricity would find its way into their cabin and their lives. They might even get an electric coffee pot. But would the coffee taste different? Thalia liked strong coffee more than Will enjoyed a strong drink. They would still have six acres, with enough room for Ollie to build his place. He had already drawn plans for a two-story log cabin. Ollie boasted to his mother, "My wife and me, whoever she is, we'll have our bedroom downstairs and three bedrooms upstairs. I want at least three, no four kids. I'll want two boys and two girls." Ollie believed raising an only child was wrong. "It ain't natural," he often said. "How can you have a family reunion without a family?"

Earlier in the day, Thalia finished a pen and ink sketch of Flatgap Baptist Church. Thalia first outlined it in pencil, trying to get it right. Draw, pause, erase, and ponder the dancing flames in the fireplace before crumpling the drawing and feeding the fire. Then tell herself, *at least it was good for something*. But she kept on and finally got it right. Thalia wished there was someone to acknowledge the accomplishment. Not to obtain approval or give it a passing grade, but for someone to recognize that it existed.

How could she overflow with talent one day, an image in her mind as clear as an October sky, her fingers working as if by magic, every stroke directed by an unseen force? The sketch drawing itself, the painting creating itself, and Thalia just going along for the ride, holding on until completion. When that occurred, exhaustion would be complete. And Thalia could exclaim, "It is finished."

At other times, she wondered if gray days simply lingered to taunt a weary soul. Sometimes, she could not even draw a chimney. After one incredibly long dry spell, she drew a picture of herself holding a massive frying pan in front of the stove. Thalia drew herself tiny, struggling to hold the pan that one could imagine weighed ninety pounds.

What was the drawing trying to say? That she was small and insignificant in the scheme of things? That the most routine and mundane things had more worth and meaning than she did?

How strange and different Will and Jesse's reaction had been to the drawing. Will smirked and said, "If this is supposed to be funny, I don't get it."

One day Jesse came to visit Hankins, who was a bit under the weather. She thought Jesse was looking for an excuse to visit, perhaps to get a hot cup of coffee and a piece of apple pie. She always sent him home with at least two big pieces, prompting Ollie to complain, "Darn, Mom, somebody already ate half the pie."

When Thalia showed Jessie the drawing, he laughed. "Thalia, this is great. You should do more of these. The women at church can relate to what you're saying."

"Jesse, exactly what am I'm saying?"

After pondering the question for a bit, Jesse replied, "If you want to draw a realistic image of yourself, draw a picture of you carrying the cabin under your arm with Will, Hankins, and Ollie's face showing out the windows. Because that's what you are, Thalia. Wherever you are, whatever you do, your spirit is a driving force."

"Oh, Jesse, hush and eat your pie," Thalia said in mock anger. Her mouth frowned, but it was impossible to misread the twinkle in her eyes.

Will arrived home around seven and made a grand entrance. "Thalia, I ain't been fair with you. I should talk with Ollie. Every time there's a tough decision to make, I leave it up to you. Things will be different after we get moved. And maybe we can start going to church again."

"It's been a while," she said softly.

"Thalia, you and Ollie didn't go with me the last time. Are you mad at that preacher about something?"

"Should I be?"

"Have you noticed he's getting more intense and louder? I'm not sure I like it."

"He has to be loud to rise above your snoring."

The new and improved Will did not last long. "See why I never try to talk to you anymore?" He strode to the pantry, grabbed a bottle, and went out on the porch.

A half-hour later, Will lurched through the door, grinned, and said, "We need to start talking more. Uh, what have you been working on today?"

Thalia reluctantly uncovered the drawing of Flatgap Baptist Church. It was a collage showing the outside of the church, the inside with the roaring pot-bellied stove with a cherry red stovepipe, a picture of the congregation, and finally Jesse Collins standing in the pulpit with clenched fists raised heavenward.

Will studied Jesse's picture a long time, running a hand across his whiskered cheeks, removing his hat and scratching his head, then shaking it sideways. "Hope you ain't trying to sell this one."

"Some I draw and paint, hoping to sell, others are keepers. Something to add to my collection. Something I do for myself."

"It don't even look like Collins. He looks too much like an angel. That sure ain't Jesse Collins. Meaner than a copperhead when he was young."

"I drew him as a man who preaches God's Word. The way heaven might see a man like that."

"Thalia, you're a strange woman."

"Will, go to bed. You'll get a headache from trying to think so much."

"Why do I even try? Wake me up at seven in the morning," Will said before slamming the bedroom door.

Thalia waited until she heard Will snoring. She pokered the fire to arouse the flames, and the fireplace pleaded for another log. Within a minute, the resurrected flames rose to defy the frosty windows. After the cabin warmed, Thalia sat on the couch and furiously sketched a picture of Will. It was not what he looked like, but tonight as she saw him. After Thalia finished the sketch, she tossed it in the fireplace and watched it burn. For some reason, she thought about the Bible passage that said, "Well done, thou good and faithful servant."

Thalia fell asleep sitting on the couch but awoke at midnight when the wind rattled the leaky window. It was chilly in the cabin again, and she threw a log in the kitchen stove and sat down at the table. When she looked out the windows, a conspiracy of stars twinkled. Something inside Thalia was astir, and she needed to get it out. She had to draw something. But what?

For as long as she could remember, she had loved art. But when she became a teenager and discovered boys, she put her ink sketches and paints and brushes back in the closet. Sometimes, she could go months without thinking about art, but then one day, a thought or mood would seize her, and she would sink in deeper than ever. The need to paint would consume her. And then it would slowly fade. And she would think, "I have no desire to paint anymore. I may never do it again." But a month or two later, it would return full force. Was it the same for everyone who loved art?

Thalia pondered Ollie's comment about wanting to have two boys and two girls. Ollie was only five when he lost his brother, who was two years younger. It took Ollie forever to grasp that Corey, his best friend, and playmate, would not return.

Yet Ollie was full of questions. Are there toys in heaven? Is Corey lonely? Can he see Jesus any time he wants? Can Corey fly? Will he ever come back? Slowly the pain faded, and Ollie's memories grew sweeter. Ollie forgot how many times Corey, attracted to his brother's Lincoln Logs set, like bees to flowers, destroyed Ollie's newly-erected cabins. After Corey passed, Thalia was so numb she could not see that Ollie was displaying a penchant for building. Some of his work revealed creativity and skill far beyond his years.

Four years later, after two miscarriages, Thalia made up her mind to never get pregnant again. She had told Jesse she knew the pregnancies were girls. Two boys and two girls, if they had survived. Exactly what Ollie had said he and his wife would have. Then she remembered that Jesse had said the same thing. But well-meaning people commented, "Sure it hurts, but it couldn't be as bad as losing little Corey." How could people be so devoid of wisdom?

Thalia remembered those years when they lived in the camp house. Ollie and his friends played in the Posers' yard on most days. The basketballs bounced erratically, footballs wobbled through icy air, and awkward wrestlers tussled.

But the maleness seeped through the cracks in the walls of the camp house, gulping air meant to be inhaled by feminine breadth. Since there was no daughter to fill the hazy void, Thalia began to paint once again, at first with joy, then zeal, then anger. How could maleness comprehend a mother's yearning for the feminine touch?

Sometimes, when Thalia saw a little girl at church dressed up like a doll, she had to fight the urge to hug the child and yell, "I want her! She's supposed to be mine!"

Thalia tried to imagine her little girl's appearance. The daughter would be a teenager now. She began to draw the child that should have had her name. Suddenly, Thalia stopped and remembered there were two miscarriages, therefore two girls, not one. A creeping sadness took over. She ripped the drawing into pieces, believing that she had somehow erased the existence of one child in favor of another. After the fire consumed every particle of the drawing, she told herself she would do it again when the time was right. Thalia believed if the little girls had lived, people would have commented, "They're different, but you can sure tell they're sisters." That is how she would draw them.

Thalia threw a massive log on the fire and stretched out on the couch again, perhaps thinking that as the flames diminished in her, a yearning ignited a secret flame elsewhere.

Chapter Seventeen

It was cold for the middle of November, but the chilled air could not bully the pot-bellied coal stove in the church house. The stove had been puffing and belching for thirty minutes, and the stovepipe was an angry red. However, with the stove door open, the energy escaped, and the puffing gradually died down.

Previously, there had been much discussion about installing a coal or oil furnace in the basement and running ductwork under the floor. But when tempers flared during a meeting, Hawthorne halted the debate and promised to resolve the issue later when cooler heads prevailed. Jesse said they would still be debating the issue when the Lord returned to gather up all the believers.

Every Sunday, before Jesse mounted the pulpit, he always felt a tingling of joy and fear. Could he rise again to the challenge? Could Jesse find the right words to share with those who needed uplifting? Sometimes after a sermon, Jesse felt that he either hit a home run or struck out with the spiritual bat on his shoulder.

Yet when Hawthorne bellowed amen the loudest, that was when Jesse thought he completely missed the spiritual target. But Jesse's preaching was not based on giving people goosebumps. Feelings rise and fall, come and go, but the Word of the Lord endured forever. Jesse had to remind himself of that now and then. However, when Hawthorne was displeased, he would say, "Sorry, Pastor, but I didn't get a thing out of the sermon today."

Jesse's reply was consistent. "Exactly what did you put into it? Did you pray before church? Did you pray before Sunday School? Did you read your Bible last night?"

The last time Jesse expressed that sentiment to Hawthorne, the deacon puffed out his jaws, folded his arms, and scowled for the entire service. Jesse smiled whenever he thought about it. Occasionally, Jesse had to remind the deacons that because the messenger was flawed, it did not mean the message was flawed.

The Poser family did not attend Sunday School this morning, but they arrived a few minutes early and sat halfway back in the middle aisle. The church held one-fifty comfortably, but this morning the deacons had to put out two dozen folding chairs in the isles.

Deacon Cartwright felt that putting out extra chairs, especially metal folding chairs, was tacky and somewhat insulting to the Lord. Jesse managed to smile when he asked Hawthorne, "If an elderly lady using a cane has to stand, will you give her your seat?"

Hawthorne had scowled and said, "Pastor Collins, remember we'll meet tomorrow night at about six. It shouldn't last long."

"Looking forward to it," the pastor half-lied while praying the meeting did not last long. When Hawthorne was angry, he always referred to Jesse as Pastor Collins and not just pastor.

Shortly before the service began, Jesse motored to the back door with short, powerful legs to greet everyone who entered the church. A handshake and a smile went a long way to make folks feel welcome, especially a stranger.

This morning Otis Winders, came shuffling through the door, avoiding eye contact with the pastor. Otis and his wife, Maylene, had been absent for two months. Maylene's mother had been in the hospital without receiving a visit from the pastor, deacons, or church members.

Jesse remembered it well. Maylene had told a church friend about her mother's condition, but the friend got her feelings hurt at an after-church gathering when someone remarked that her fried chicken, although tasty, was a tad greasy. She played hooky for the next two weeks until the pastor realized she had been absent and promptly called her. She returned to church the following Sunday but forgot about her conversation with Maylene.

"Otis, good to see you this morning. How's your lovely wife?" Jesse said.

"Fair, just fair."

"Well, tell her we miss her. Also, I'd like to visit her mother as soon as I can. Would you go with me?"

"I'll have to think about it," Otis replied, refusing to look at the pastor. Otis was still pouting.

The last person to enter the church was Abe Drubbard. Abe had given his life to the Lord three years earlier after struggling with the bottle. A month ago, Abe told Jesse that he had been strangling the bottle's neck, and a demon was living in his head rent-free.

Jesse quickly deduced that Abe had been drinking heavily and was depressed. Abe and his wife had split up and reunited twice the past year. Abe said they could not live together, but neither wanted to live apart. Jesse suggested marriage counseling, and Abe quickly agreed, but Coleen would not budge. "Coleen says it's all my fault, and she don't need no counseling," Abe later informed Jesse.

Jesse knew of Coleen, and so did a lot of other men. Two years ago, when Abe asked Coleen to marry him, she replied, "I want to pick out my ring. A diamond. A big one." Jesse wanted to shake Abe's shoulders and say, "Are you crazy? You'll never have a minute of peace. You deserve better." But all Jesse said was, "Have you prayed and asked God if this is the right one? Could God have someone else in mind? Please pray about it."

Abe grunted an unclear reply and never came for the two pre-marital counseling sessions that Jesse always recommended. When Jesse saw them in church a month later, Coleen had a ring on her wedding finger, the diamond the size of a hickory nut. Eight months later, they separated for the first time.

Last week Hawthorne told Jesse that a church member recently saw Abe exiting a bar in Crooked Creek. The good deacon wanted Abe disciplined, but Jesse believed a hug or two from the church members would go a lot farther.

Before Jesse closed the church door, he said, "Abe, let's go to lunch on Saturday. There's a barbeque restaurant that just opened in Crooked Creek, and everybody says it's great." Abe almost smiled and nodded yes. *Lunch and encouraging words worked wonders*, Jesse told himself as he hustled down the aisle and onto the podium.

"Good morning, and God bless you. Sister Sara Hatfield will play a few songs on the piano this morning. So we'll all close our eyes and pray that the Holy Spirit will join us thus in celebrating our risen Lord and Savior, Jesus Christ."

The long-legged, rail-thin, and wobbly Wallace Foreacre had led the music for sixteen years. This morning he jump-started the service with songs straight from the recently acquired songbooks. The songs were a blessing. "The Old

Rugged Cross" and "Blessed Assurance" and a piece to get the spiritual blood flowing, "I'll Fly Away."

Jesse preached long and loud that morning and repeatedly hit hard with scripture about wisdom. His sermon centered around Proverbs 3:13: "Happy is the man that findeth wisdom and the man that getteth understanding."

"No matter how much you own, or how much your fellow man respects you, or how much knowledge you possess, if you lack wisdom, you'll make the wrong decision every time."

Jesse then told a story that had been in his family forever. Every time the story was a little different, but the theme remained the same.

Years ago, a man in Harlan County had a garden that was the envy of everybody. The man was not just born with a green thumb; he was green as grass all over. People came from all over Harlan County to see his garden. Everybody asked him his secret, but he just laughed and said, "I listen to the plants' talk. They tell me what they need, and I give it to them."

But it takes years of practice to hear a plant talk. It does not come easy. But the gardener refused to share his secret despite many folks having stubborn gardens because of the poor soil.

Before long, it was time to harvest his bountiful crop. But the man had a problem. He could not make up his mind where to start. Day after day, he would begin to pick something but stop and rest a spell. Everything was so beautiful he could not decide where to begin.

He changed his mind a hundred times. He started to pick the tomatoes, then jumped to the corn, the beans, the squash, the peas, the potatoes, and the melons. Finally, he grew weary and sat down under a shade tree to ponder his dilemma.

He sat under that shade tree all summer and fall and failed to pick the first bean. Meanwhile, everything rotted on the vine. Word got around that he was touched in the head, and people came from all over the county to see for themselves. They laughed and said he had a gourd for a head, but he just replied, "You don't understand. You don't understand at all." One day he got up early, set his fields on fire, and went into the woods. No one ever saw him again.

Today, nothing grows in those fields, not even briars. Folks say that you can see him walking in those fields late at night. And during harvest, if you look closely, you'll see him sitting under that shade tree every time the moon's out.

When the pastor concluded his story, silence thick as molasses settled over the congregation. Jesse spoke so softly even the squirming children stopped moving to listen. "God gives us talents and abilities to use to help others. If we fail to help others, our gift will wither and die. God gives us the wisdom to use those gifts. Now let's bow our heads and pray for wisdom."

When the Poser family exited the church, they stopped and complimented Jesse on the sermon. Ollie was the last one to leave. He almost shook Jesse's hand but withdrew it at the last second.

"Pastor, you said some older folks got a house that needed fixing. I reckon I can help, so let me know when." Thalia smiled.

Chapter Eighteen

Hankins was half-asleep in his rocker when footsteps, heavy and stiff-legged, marched across the front porch and an awkward hand tapped the door. Hankins considered fetching his pistol but decided it was not worth the effort. It was in the nightstand by his bed in the smaller bedroom. He chose to sleep there because it was the room where Sarah spent her last night on earth.

When a voice called out, "Old man, don't you get out of bed before noon?" Hankins grinned and moved his feet fast, although he did not cover much ground. It was his friend, Chester Wiggins.

Hankins jerked the doorknob three times before the door opened. The damp air had swollen the door, and Hankins would have to get Ollie to trim it down. "Chester, what in the world are you doing up so early? Did the slats fall out of the bed?"

"I'd feel better if they did. My back is getting the best of me since the weather chilled."

"Have a seat while I fix coffee. Do you want breakfast? I ain't eat yet. Just been up a short while, rocking and reading my Bible."

"You always did go after the Word even when you were meaner than a chained dog."

"How's your brother? The last time I talked to him, he acted like he hardly knew me."

"Roy's getting worse. It's been two years since Bessie passed away, but he's still mourning."

Roy and Bessie had been a mystery. Hardly a day passed without them fussing and fighting. They acted like they could not stand to be around one another. But they stayed together forty-four years. "And Roy can't catch his breath," Chester added. "All that coal dust. A wonder any of us can breathe."

"Ain't that the truth. But the companies claim coal dust don't hurt the lungs. I guess moonshine can make the same claim."

While the coffee perked, Hankins eased into his chair but did not rock. Funny how the least thing plunged him back into the past. He could clearly remember things from long ago, but the other day when he hunted for his pipe, the darn thing was stuck in his shirt pocket. He thought about the old gospel song, "Precious Memories, How They Linger." Indeed, they were precious, and Lord, they had certainly lingered.

Hankins understood the heartache of losing a loved one. Sarah passed away unexpectedly at age forty. She had not been sick, just feeling a bit tired and dizzy-headed, she told Hankins before she retired at nine that Saturday night. Hankins said he would be to bed shortly. He wanted to reread his Sunday School lesson and polish his church shoes. An hour later, he eased into bed, trying not to wake Sarah, and kissed her on the cheek. She sighed and rolled onto her side and snored for a spell. That was the last sound he heard her make.

And it happened just when things had gotten better. Hankins had been working steadily for seven months, the pantry was full of canned goods, their three boys had a new pair of boots, and they had saved eighty-five dollars they kept in a King Edward cigar box in a cedar chest. Their hard-luck fund, they had called it.

Good times and bad times. No matter how alert Hankins had been to the signs, it always came as a surprise. He might work overtime one week, and the next week arrive at work and see a sign posted at the bathhouse entrance that announced "Closed Until Further Notice." Hankins had repeatedly advised younger folks to be prepared. "Bad times always catch a good man with his britches down," Hankins often lectured.

On three different occasions, after two massive layoffs and a mine closing and Hankins unemployment pay running out, he journeyed north to Cincinnati. The first two times, Hankins left Sarah behind and said for her to expect a money order in the mail from his first paycheck.

To this day, Hankins hated the color pink-always the color of a layoff slip. Why not black for coal? Why not white for neutral? Why a pretty color that Sarah liked to have in the house? The gentle color did not ease the pain of losing a job when the average family could not scrape together twenty dollars.

One boss seemed to enjoy handing out pink slips. He never quite smiled, but he would come close. On many occasions, an angry miner would say, "If he smiles when he hands me that pink slip, he'll be wearing store-bought teeth the next week."

And it was always on Friday and without any warning. When Hankins received the dreaded slip for the third time, he avoided looking at it and forced himself to look past the boss and stare at an unpainted spot on the concrete block wall where a bulletin board once hung.

That night, Hankins sat on his front porch swing until Sarah went to bed. When he felt all alone, he reread the pink slip, carefully folded it, and put it in his Bible on the fireplace mantle.

A month later, Hankins sold everything and put three dollars gas in a forty-eight Hudson, piled his mining equipment in the kitchen corner of the camp house, used a wire coat hanger to secure the car's muffler, and left without locking the doors.

The car was held together with mostly wire and prayer as they began their journey to Cincinnati. But this time, Hankins took Sarah, Clete, and Jasper with him. "We ain't never moving back," Hankins said unconvincingly.

When they left Hoedown, the sky was painted black. Did the moon and stars hide in shame for what happened? As Hankins passed through Lexington, the sun came up, and he thought about his Bible, where he had left the pink slip. Suddenly, he stopped worrying. Hankins hid the pink slip on the page with his favorite Bible verse: "Be still and know that I am God."

A week later, five other couples from around Hoedown loaded up what little they had and headed north in a caravan of clunkers. Hankins had sent back word that factory jobs were available. All the families moved close to the factories in a section called Norwood. It seemed like half the people who settled there were from eastern Kentucky.

One winter night, Hankins, longing for home and needing to hear some country music, grabbed his coat, hat, and knife and kissed Sarah goodbye. Encouraged by a February wind at his back, he half-ran to a corner bar. As soon as he entered the bar, a couple of rough-looking characters started giving him the eye.

Hankins told himself he was too tired for such foolishness. But Hankins decided if he had to fight, it would be the bigger one. The bigger man looked strong but slow, and his eyes suggested he would not stand toe to toe and slug it out. Hankins figured he would whip the big man, and the little man would back off unless he was stupid. Then Hankins would insist on buying both of them a beer, and that would end it.

Haskins stood up and said, "If you're wanting to bump heads, just say the word."

The smaller man said, "You sound like you're from back home."

"Hoedown in Harlan County. Rather be home, but the mine shut down. To keep living indoors, I ended up here."

The bartender guffawed and said, "I figured he's one of us, not backing down." It turned out half the men in the bar were from either Cumberland, Harlan, or Hazard. And those two rascals were cousins from Pineknot, in neighboring Letcher County.

Two months later, Roy and Bessie, with no kids in tow, moved out of Sarah and Hankins's large apartment and rented a two-room apartment above the bar. But they continued to fight. Now and then, the bartender, who was from Crooked Creek, would climb atop the pool table and jab the ceiling and with a broom handle to stop the racket. The local pool shark claimed he could not hear the pool balls banging for all the ruckus.

Hankins wondered why people who fussed the most tended to stick it out. One day, in exasperation, Hankins said, "Roy, if you and Bessie can't stand each other, why don't you split up?"

"Good Lord," Roy had squalled. "When Bessie spent two nights in the hospital, I hardly slept a wink. I ain't never been afraid to grapple with any man in Harlan County, but I was skittish all night long and slid the shotgun under the bed so I could get some rest. She's the only woman I ever courted. Besides, I ain't kissed but three girls my whole life."

Sarah and Hankins had grown weary of moving back and forth. But when a big company bought out a bunch of smaller mines and expanded mining operations, Hankins and Sarah headed south on Interstate seventy-five. That was the last time they had to leave eastern Kentucky.

By the time the next round of layoffs occurred, the miners had voted in the United Mineworkers labor union. The miners gained the right to bid on job openings at the company's other mines. Chester, Roy, and Hankins now had enough seniority under their belts to keep them working. That was good because Sarah soon gave birth to a third son and named him Will.

"Hankins, you ever wonder how life might've been if you'd stayed in Cincinnati?"

"I've thought about it some. But I'd just made the same mistakes again. Something about these mountains kept pulling me back."

Chester chuckled and said, "You start out hating coal mining and end up not wanting to do anything else. But I sure hated midnight shift. My wife would pack my lunch bucket and suitcase, sit both by the back door, and tell me to take my pick. If I knew then what I know now, I'd picked the suitcase."

Hankins understood how Chester felt. Hankins detested the second shift because he left for work before the kids got home from school. The kids were in bed when Hankins arrived home at night. It seemed like they were grown before he realized it.

Although Clete was two years older than Jasper, Clete started school late and failed fourth grade. So when Clete graduated high school, Jasper, a junior, quit school. They both were ready to earn some money but wanted nothing to do with a coal mine. The day they left to go north, it hit Hankins like a sledgehammer. For years he fretted about working all that overtime. But when a man had a houseful to feed, what could he do?

Things were easier when the miners voted the union in. Hankins got forty cents, and Chester got a quarter an hour raise. But Chester fussed about it for the next ten years. No matter how many times Hankins explained that roof bolters made more than shuttle car drivers because the work was harder and more dangerous, it never penetrated Chester's head.

"Hankins, you remember when the company signed a union contract, and we got letters from John L. Lewis. I thought I was the only one and showed it to everybody. Come to find out there were about two hundred of those letters floating around."

What happened to all those years. How could they slip away so quickly? Chester, Roy, and Hankins had talked for years about visiting the union's headquarters in Washington, DC, located just a few blocks from the White House. But they never made it there, nor to Florida to go deep-sea fishing, or even to see the Kentucky Derby in Louisville.

Hankins always wondered why they never fulfilled those dreams. Maybe when they finally got the time and money, they could not remember why they had wanted to go.

"Chester, didn't you meet John L. Lewis one time?"

"I sure did. I wish to God somebody had a camera that day. I was in the hospital the first time I hurt my back. He came to Harlan to dedicate the Miners' Memorial Hospital. He came to my room and shook my hand. He said what we accomplished would benefit generations to come. I got tears in my eyes, and I never was one to cry. I hardly cried over Chester Junior getting killed. But they said I was in shock."

"How long has it been?"

"Eighteen years this September. But it was different this year."

"How so?"

"I'm ashamed to say I forget about it. I had a doctor's appointment that day and had to get my truck fixed. The dang carburetor was acting up. Do you think it was wrong for me to forget?"

"Lord, Chester, eighteen years is a mighty long time."

"I dreamed about junior last week."

"About him getting covered up in that roof fall?"

"No, I dreamed he was sitting at the foot of my bed just staring at me. When he was a kid, I'd blister his britches if he got in trouble, and somebody else told me first. So when he'd done wrong, he'd wake me up and tell me. In my dream, I asked him why he had to leave, and he just vanished."

"Junior was a good boy. He would've made a fine young man."

"I believe so. But Junior was shy with the girls, not like his old man."

"Chester, if you'd been a little shyer, you might've stayed married."

"Well, there's nothing wrong with liking women. My problem was I liked too many at one time."

"I'm getting hungry. Want some breakfast?"

"No, I better run. Got to check on Roy."

"It's always something."

"Ain't it, though," Chester said and sat down his empty coffee cup.

Chapter Nineteen

"Mildred, I'm meeting with Deacon Cartwright this morning," Pastor Collins said as he filled his coffee mug. Thursday, for some reason, was the pastor's favorite day of the week. Fewer visitors and hours of quiet to prepare Sunday's sermon. But so far, Jesse had trouble coming up with an idea, and he desperately needed to pray.

"Pastor, here's a check for the repairs on the Wooten's house. A hundred dollars won't go far on that shack. They need a better place to live. Besides, you'll need an army tank to make it up Wooten Hollow."

"If it takes more money, I'll pay out of my pocket."

"Pastor Collins, you got a better heart than a head."

"Well, Mildred, we can't have it all," Jesse replied.

"Get Hawthorne to help out. He's got more money than the governor."

"No doubt he's well off. It's a wonder you never let him court you."

"I'd rather live in a coal bin. Hawthorne could make Saint Peter cuss on Sunday."

"Sister, I'm going to my office and pray for a spell. Send Hawthorne in when he gets here."

It was easy to find fault with Deacon Cartwright, but he deserved an A for promptness. One minute before nine, he was tapping lightly on the pastor's office door. Hawthorne wore a bright red necktie with his dark gray suit. He would not enter a church without wearing a suit. "We're supposed to give out best to the Lord," he always said when someone questioned him about his attire.

Mildred once asked Hawthorne if he dressed like that when he went to the horse races in Lexington to gamble. Hawthorne was insulted. "Mildred, I find your attempt at humor falls far short of levity."

"You mean I ain't funny?" she said.

When Hawthorne entered Jesse's office, he said, "How did the folks like the new songs books. I believe the quality is superb."

"They loved them. The lyrics are in big print and easy to read. You did a fine job. I'll send the pastor a letter of thanks."

"No need for concern. I've already done it. I assumed you would be appreciative. And now on to the business at hand."

"Indeed," Jesse said with a twinkle in his eye. He felt playful this morning. However, Jesse knew that the devout deacon wanted to talk about some folks in the church who had stumbled recently.

"Pastor, have you talked to Abe Drubbard about his drinking?"

Jesse inhaled and exhaled deeply and gulped his coffee before speaking. He wanted to choose his words carefully. "I took Abe to lunch, and he spilled his guts. He's tried to stop drinking on his own, but he can't do it."

"Well done, Pastor."

"But I told him that none of us are without sin and that we all have weaknesses that the devil exploits. I said he needed his church family to surround him in prayer and encouragement."

"A drunkard in our midst?"

"People accused Jesus of being a friend of sinners."

"I suppose so, but what about Jobelle Honeycutt? She's been seen in the company of Luke Slaughter, whose divorce isn't final. I got it from a most reliable source."

"You mean Doak Owens?"

"Well, yes, as a matter of fact, it was Doak. A bit of a busybody but most reliable in all details."

"I had a chance to talk to Luke. His wife left him and moved to Texas four years ago. He can't find her to give her divorce papers. I invited him to church. He said we'd have to timber up the roof if he showed up. I said we got some good roof bolters here in the congregation. He laughed and said he just might show up one day."

"What about this illicit affair with Jobelle?"

"She has to care for three kids. Luke fixed her car and repaired the back steps at her house. He wouldn't even let her pay him."

"I bet he's using those back steps quite a bit, especially at night."

Jesse was a teakettle that had been sitting on a gas burner too long. He slammed both hands on the desk and said, "The church is the only army that shoots its wounded. Someone spread a rumor about her, and she's hurt. Jobelle said she'd never be caught dead in a church again. For God's sake, show some mercy."

"Pastor, I know you mean well, but you a bit lax."

"Let's move on to another subject, or this meeting is over."

"Very well. Your sermon Sunday night was most excellent. Very clever the way you worked another message into the message."

"I'm confused. I thought my sermon was that if God blesses us, we should help the less fortunate."

"You mean it wasn't a somewhat subtle reference to the coal company's interest in buying property. The company's approached some church members about selling their land. Are you aware of this?"

"Several members asked me about it. I said they should seek the advice of someone with a good head for business."

"Also, some members think we should sell the church property. The company has offered good money for land that is unsuitable for farming. Besides, our church is too far from town to get some of the more affluent members."

"I've heard a rumor, but it takes a church vote to sell. I'm opposed to it. The people in these hills need a church they can get to in the winter months. It wouldn't be fair to them."

"Pastor, are you averse to progress?"

"It's according to what you mean by progress. I own eight acres, and I'm not selling a square inch."

"I believe MMR would be greatly interested in your land at an attractive price."

"If I would do something for them?"

"Well, uh, yes."

"Just out of curiosity, have you been in touch with Will Poser?"

"I'm under no obligation whatsoever to divulge my sources."

"That's what I thought."

"Pastor, I must object. We've been at odds ever since you shoved me against a wall that time. Ten members left the church because of you."

"Actually, two families moved up north, one became a pastor, and another member's family moved him to a nursing home in Harlan."

"If you're going to nitpick, you are correct. But assaulting a deacon with an impeccable record of decorum is appalling."

"Hawthorne, I love the way you express yourself."

"I would have filed charges, but I wanted to avoid hurting the church. It's this kind of incident that tears a church apart."

"Didn't Pastor Coltrane punch you one time? And what about that man named Glover Ratliff who moved to Hazard a few years ago? Didn't he choke you during an argument about whether to hold a foot washing in May or October?"

"Despicable!"

"I offered to resign, but the deacons voted four to one for me to stay. Wonder who cast a vote against me?"

"I'm not at liberty to divulge such information."

"I'm not proud of losing my temper, but you said I was having an affair with a married woman."

"Pastor, I was simply investigating the matter. I simply reported the talk I'd heard. I never really believed it."

"I was engaged to Thalia Poser many years ago. Her father disapproved of me, so I moved away. I returned when my mother died. I've never misbehaved toward Thalia. If Will or Ollie knew what you said, you would've had to move to Tennessee."

"I'll never leave Harlan County."

"Hawthorne, you're still angry and bitter and hurting, aren't you?"

"Yes, I suppose. Myra's been gone nine years, and I still expect her there when I get home from church on Sunday night."

"I'm sorry, Hawthorne. I know you loved her very much."

"Myra left the day after my youngest son graduated high school. She left with a bum who didn't even have a good muffler on the truck he stole her away in."

Hawthorne squeezed his fists and squalled in agony. Jesse stepped toward Hawthorne and hugged him. Completely surprised by Jesse's display of affection, Hawthorne coughed several times before regaining his composure. "Uh, you've seen the dam that MMR is building at the head of the hollow. If the dam ever broke, our little church might float away like Noah's Ark."

"Should we talk to the company?"

"We discussed it at a deacons' meeting while you were away."

"You had no right. I'm supposed to be there when you meet."

"Pastor, just think about a new church building, a much larger membership, and a better salary for you. A good move all the way around."

"Isn't there a two-acre tract of land across the street from your grocery store where a church burned down years ago? Doesn't one of your sons-in-law own that land?"

"Says who?"

"Doak Owens."

"Blasted blabbermouth. But still, it's something to think about."

"Hawthorne, you've given me a great deal to think about."

Chapter Twenty

The 88,000 miles on Jesse's '56 pickup truck were hard-earned miles over rock-pitted roads, across trickling streams, and up hills, so steep a mountain goat would have stumbled at some point. Where the road narrowed, cliffs abounded, and the level road was muddy. It was not a gentle environment for the faint-hearted, but the Wooten family managed to tough it out for two decades. Jesse marveled that the people who struggled were often unaware of how much they lacked.

Both truck windows were down and Ollie, with a plum-sized cud of tobacco nestled in his left cheek, spit powerfully out the window. "Pastor, I thought we were going to roll back a time or two. You need to think about getting you a good mule."

"I wouldn't get much of a trade-in on a good mule," Jesse laughed. There was something about Ollie that made Jesse want to grab the boy and hug him to death. He had a lot of his mother in him. Unfortunately, a part of Will also dwelled within. Opposites may attract, but sometimes the pull of opposing forces can cause inertia. Jesus had preached that a man could not serve two masters. Maybe that was part of Ollie's problem, and he ended up rejecting both parent's guidance.

Jesse had seen it happen to other young men like Zebulon and Twilla Thompkins's son, Zeb Jr. His mother wanted him to become a preacher, the father, a coal miner.

Zeb chose neither path and became a thief. However, Zeb Jr. recently told his parents he would become a new man after his parole in two years.

"Ollie, have you decided what to do this coming year?"

"I'm not going back to high school. I'll get my diploma through that vocational school over in Harlan. Besides, what's it to you?"

"Your mother is worried about you."

"You're always talking to Mom about something, ain't you?"

"Ollie, I'm your mother's pastor."

"Yeah, right. You think I don't know? You think I'm stupid?"

"Ollie, that's not fair, and you know it."

"Relax, preacher man. Mom thinks the world of you, and so does grandad. Dad, not so much."

"Now you listen to me real good. I'd never do anything to hurt your mother."

"That's obvious. If someone hurt Mom, you'd throw them off a cliff. I'm not saying it's a bad thing. I'm just saying I know."

"Ollie, unfortunately, you know very little." Jesse felt the way he did when trying to reason with Deacon Cartwright. Jesse's mind shifted back to the job at hand when his truck greeted another pothole, and the entire load shifted in the truck's bed. He was glad they were almost there. "Ollie, you think we've got enough material to do the job?"

"Can't say until I see the place for myself. Why in the world are they stuck way up here?"

"They have nowhere else to go."

"We'll see when we get there. But I ain't doing nothing halfway."

"Ollie, I'm handy with a hammer, but I don't have the skills you have. You take charge."

"Good, I'll enjoy bossing a pastor around. But look, Jesse, about Mom, there ain't a problem you liking my mom for a friend. I'm glad she's got somebody she can talk to about stuff. But when she looks at you, she smiles all over. I think it's kind of funny."

The yard was level where they unloaded a dozen plywood sheets, two dozen one-by-fours, concrete blocks, and rolls of felt material. They left a wide assortment of tools in the truck bed. After they climbed ten rickety steps onto a warped front porch, Ollie said, "These steps have to go."

Sister Elvie Wooten greeted them at the door of a ramshackle house that was desperate for repairs. "Pastor, I just fixed us a pot of coffee, and who's this handsome young man you brought with you?"

Ollie blushed. For all his bravado, Ollie was bashful. "Sister Wooten, this is Ollie Poser. Son of Thalia and Will Poser. You know them?"

Sister Wooten scrunched her brow, trying to remember. "The name rings a bell. But at my age, everything rings a bell, but none too clearly. Pastor, what have you planned for today?"

"I'm not sure. Ollie is heading up the project. Don't let his youth fool you. He can fix anything."

They both turned to Ollie, and he blushed again. "Mam, I reckon I'd like to look underneath the house to make sure everything's alright. Then I'll check outside the house."

Sister Wooten said, "Plenty of height underneath, but lower on the back end. There's a door on the far side of the house. And Ollie, God bless you for helping us. You don't know how much it means to Charles and me."

"Uh, Charles, that your husband, Mam?"

"Charles is my brother, and he's bedridden. He's sleeping right now. He's doing poorly."

Ten minutes later, Ollie returned and sat down at the kitchen table and began to draw, erase, and draw again. Jesse glanced at the page filled with hen scratches of numbers and half-written words the pastor could not decipher. Ollie filled two pages of notes, smiled, and looked up, and almost whispered, "Mam, could I have that cup of coffee before we get started?"

Ollie was bounding with energy and could not wait to begin. Ollie had found a wide assortment of lumber under the house. There were pre-cut sides for the steps for the front porch. The rough-oak two-by-twelves were not precise cuts but were long enough to do the job. Ollie ripped off a wobbly banister rail and proclaimed, "Here's where the new steps will go. It'll only take five steps instead of ten. A lot safer to get up and down for older folks."

Meanwhile, Jesse almost daintily carried the material up the wobbly steps, toting two thick plywood sheets at a time, while Ollie built the new steps. Ollie was impressed. The short, bulky preacher was stout as a bull. Ollie told himself he would hate to tangle with Jesse if the pastor was angry.

After Jesse put the lumber on the front porch, Ollie said, "You won't believe this, but somebody must've worked for the railroad. There's a dozen ties under there. A bit warped, but that creosote keeps them forever. Let's get under the floor, Pastor, er, I mean Jesse."

The ramshackle house, about eight hundred square feet, had severe sags in all the floors. However, the clay soil was hard as concrete underneath the house, and timbering with the railroad ties was easy. Jesse handled the railroad ties as if they were popular wood, and they stood almost as straight as an arrow. Ollie then drove cap wedges above the ties making the floor creak and snap but yield. It would take an earth-quake to dislodge the railroad ties.

Six railroad ties later, Ollie stepped back to admire their work. Then they cut and nailed two dozen cross pieces between the floor joists to make them sturdier. "Jesse, it takes longer doing it right, but it's worth it." He took pride in his work.

Back inside the house, Ollie said, "Mam, was your hus-band a railroad man? Those railroad ties are great for sup-port. All kinds of good wood under there, too."

"Beck, my husband did a little bit of everything. Mining, railroading, factory work, farming. He did about everything but sell shoes. But it seemed like if he went to work some-where, the place would close the next month. Beck always said he was jinxed. It seemed like the faster he ran away from a hornet's nest, the quicker he'd run into a briar patch. But he never quit. He never gave up; his heart just gave out."

"I'm sorry, Mam. I surely am." Jesse was pleased. He knew it would not take long for Ollie to warm up to Elvie Wooten.

While Ollie drank his coffee, Jesse was in the back room talking to Charles. He could hear Jesse laughing about some-thing. When Ollie finished his coffee Sister Wooten said, "Ollie, go say hello to Charles. He likes to get visitors."

Ollie reluctantly entered a dark and dreary bedroom, where a grizzled old man lay in a narrow bed in a narrow bedroom and had his back propped up with several pillows. When Charles saw Ollie, his eyes widened, and he began to wave his arms in spastic jerks and uttered what sounded like gibberish. Ollie felt like running from the room when Jesse said, "Ollie, say hello to Brother Charles."

"Uh, uh, Mr. Wooten."

Charles cut loose with a string of words that made Ollie back away. Ollie was ashamed that he felt so uncomfortable. If Ollie could just understand what Charles was saying. "He said God bless you for helping fix their house," Jesse explained. Ollie fled the room.

Five minutes later, Ollie and Jesse were tacking the felt material on the sides of the house. Next, they nailed one by four strips of wood, sixteen inches apart, to attach the plywood. "Jesse, the north side of the house gets hit hardest by the weather. If we don't get nothing else done, we got to get this fixed." After Ollie and Jesse installed the plywood siding on the north side of the house, they broke for lunch.

It was bright and sunny and fifty degrees, so they ate lunch outside. When Ollie uncovered his lunch tray that Sister Wooten prepared, he was shocked. Fried chicken, potato salad, baked beans, cornbread, and a hot mug of coffee greeted him.

After saying grace, Jesse tore into his food with relish, but Ollie refused to take a bite. "Don't you like fried chicken? It's almost as good as your mother's cooking."

"They can't afford to feed us like this. I ain't eating a bite."

"Ollie, if we don't eat this meal, Sister Wooten will be hurt bad. Let them help the best they can. Please don't take this away from them."

Ollie began eating but reluctantly. Finally, he said, "I guess you're right. You've got a decent head on your shoulders for a preacher. I thought most everybody in the church was like Deacon Cartwright."

"Ollie, you reckon we can get the siding on before dark?" Jesse held the tongue and grooved plywood that snapped into place, and Ollie did the nailing. The job took two hours, and

Ollie stood back to admire their work. "Jesse, when we get all the siding done, they'll be warm as toast this winter."

"Ollie, this is good work. I don't know how to thank you."

"Then don't. But I was wondering what kind of heat the Wooten's use?"

"Coal when they've got it. Otherwise, a lot of wood."

"I saw a stack of pine logs near the back door. Pine burns up too quick. Creosote will build up in a chimney enough to burn a house down if you ain't careful. Has the chimney ever been cleaned?"

"I cleaned it last year, and it was bad."

"Tell you what. I've cleaned and repaired our chimney three times. I've got the tools, and I'll do it tomorrow."

"You're coming back tomorrow?"

"Yeah, let's get it done. I've got a ton of firewood cut. I'll bring a pickup load of oak in Dad's truck. That way, you'll have room to carry more plywood. I'd say another eight sheets with what's under the floor will do it. Remember, get the tongue and groove with the rough texture because it holds up better. And make sure it's for the outdoors. Cost a dollar more a sheet, but it's worth it."

"Ollie, I had something else planned tomorrow."

"Cancel it. We got to get this siding on before the first snow."

Jesse grabbed Ollie in a bear hug and said, "If I had a son, I'd want him to be just like you."

"Right, Jesse. Don't fall apart on me now and start preaching a sermon. So far, it's been a good day, so don't mess it up."

As they drove back down Wooten Hollow, Jesse could hardly contain himself. "Ollie, you're a perfectionist. But that's a good thing for work like you do."

"I guess I take after Mom. She'll draw something and tear it up a half-dozen times until she gets it right. It has to be her best before she puts her name on something. But I'm guessing you'd know that."

As the night, dark as ink, blighted the truck's path down the hollow, the wind picked up and rattled the door's windows. Jesse turned on the heater, but it made little difference because the temperature had dropped to forty degrees. Jesse feared if the temperature dropped ten more degrees, it would snow. Jesse wanted to play the radio but then remembered it had not worked in over a year. *One more year, and I'm getting me a newer truck,* Jesse told himself. But the thought of owing anyone a nickel almost made him angry.

He looked at Ollie, whose head rested against the passenger's window, and he was snoring lightly. He would give anything to be a friend to this young man. But Jesse was afraid that he would grow to love him like his own son. There was so much love inside Jesse he was not quite sure what to do with it. But tonight, Jesse Collins was happier than he had been in a long time.

Chapter Twenty-One

Will was despondent after meeting with Clive McAlister. Will told Clive that few members were in favor of selling the church's property. The superintendent then wrapped himself in his executive cloak and started calling Will Mr. Poser. "So it's no longer Will since you've got a clear title to the land," Will retorted. Clive did not reply. But Clive did say earlier that MMR had changed plans again and would not move the cabin until late summer. But that was fine with Will. It gave him more time to decide how to break the news to Ollie.

When Will drove past the old home place, ghosts from the past, some good, some bad, reached out and grabbed him. He stopped along aside the road and looked at their old yard. It looked half the size of when he was a child.

He immediately conjured up a memory. He could see himself running with a football and Jasper tackling him too hard, knocking the breath out of him. As always, Clete came to Will's defense. "Dang it, Jasper, he ain't but ten. You treat him like he's a teenager."

"Toughen him up," Jasper chuckled.

"I'll toughen you up," Clete replied with a slap across the top of Jasper's head. And so it began—a fistfight between two brothers. Despite Clete being two years older, Jasper gave a good account of himself. While they slugged it out, Will, unharmed, began to cry, prompting both brothers to stop suddenly. "What's he crying for?" Jasper said. "Ain't nobody touched him."

"Shut up," Clete said.

"Make me," Jasper replied. And the fight resumed until the shouts of neighborhood children alerted Hankins of yet another boyhood battle. Hankins could identify the sound of shouts when it was a fight. It was like him knowing the sound of an unstable roof when he tapped it with a hammer. It made a distinct sound that he could not explain.

Hankins stomped out on the front porch, the Bible in one hand and his pipe in the other. "I'll take my belt to both of you. If you can't play without fighting, you can help your mother clean the house and wash dishes." Clete and Jasper immediately shook hands. Jasper told Will he was sorry, but when he turned his back, Will threw the rock-hard football, hitting his brother in the back of the head, and then ran like his pants were afire.

Meanwhile, neighborhood boys who came to watch the fight immediately grew bored after the truce was enacted and fled along with Will. As they scattered down the road, they yelled, "Sissy, sissy, Jasper and Clete wash dishes." Clete had to restrain Jasper, who was proficient at teasing but was devoid of any tolerance when he was the target.

Will had often criticized his dad for what he called wallowing in the past. But Will did the same thing every time he saw the old home place. Will decided he would not visit his father today. Will needed to be alone. It had finally hit Will that most of the Poser land now belonged to a coal company. And the $40,000, instead of being a blessing, was a burden. At first, the money made him want to shout out loud, but now it depressed him. He could not bring himself to spend a penny. The better off the family was financially, the more unhappy he had become.

He needed a beer. He would go back to Ed's Place. It was the most depressing bar in the county, but he would not run into anyone he knew. Will was trying to figure out how something could cause him joy one day and sadness the next day.

When Will entered the bar, it looked even more run-down than just a few weeks ago. He sat at a booth and noticed that the big guy, Dan, was back again. But something was different this time. Dan leaped to his feet and swaggered across the floor, head up, shoulders erect, long arms dangling far from his side, swinging as if they possessed a will of their own. He radiated the good-natured cockiness of someone who had just won a new set of snow tires in a January raffle.

Dan and his friend Gary sat at a booth with another man and woman, and all four shared a laugh. Will tried not to overhear, but Gary's voice carried all over the barroom. Dan and a bully named Burle had finally tangled, and Dan knocked him out. Also, Dan now had a girlfriend who was crazy about him.

The more they laughed, the sadder Will became. He decided one beer would be his limit, but then Carla walked through the door. He had not seen her in years, but she still looked good. Her auburn hair was somewhat darker than twenty years ago, making her look older, not younger.

On many nights Will wondered if he should have stuck with her instead of making a move for Thalia. Will had always thought Thalia pretty, even though a bit scrawny, but once Jesse was out of the picture, she looked even better. Will had not been afraid of Jesse Collins. However, the few people who had tangled with Jesse during their youth seemed to limp a long time afterward. When he heard that Jesse was gone for good, Will got a haircut and a new flannel shirt and went courting.

Will overheard Carla ask the bartender if she could use their phone, and he replied, "Yeah, we got one, but it ain't worked in two days. Sorry, lady."

Carla thrust her hands on her hips and said, "But I've got a flat tire." Will stood, picked up his beer, quickly drained it, and followed Carla out the door. The beer sign above the door flickered goodbye.

Outside, Carla had opened her car's trunk and was staring at something. "Hello, Carla," Will said.

Alarmed, she grabbed a tire iron and whirled around but stopped quickly and smiled in relief. "Will Poser, what in the world are you doing in this dump? I thought you were living high on the hog."

"Don't believe everything you hear."

"Anyway, you're an answer to a prayer. Mind fixing my flat?"

After Will tossed the flat tire in the trunk, he said, "Carla, looks like you hit something and ruined the tire, and your spare is nothing to brag about."

"In other words, I need new tires."

"Buy two new tires and put them on the front, and you'll be in good shape."

Carla said, "I'll buy you a beer for this. You're a lifesaver."

"I need to get home."

"Oh, that's right. You're a married man, ain't you? Didn't you marry that tall girl that was always painting something? But just how married are you anyway?"

Will was unsure how to answer the question. The bloom was off the rose a bit, but Carla was still attractive. Well, cute anyway, and petite. She had married a man the size of a lineman for a professional football team, but he had died young, and she raised two children all by herself. He had to respect her for that.

"Will, do you ever think about you and me, and what if?"

"I have from time to time. Everybody has doubts. Everybody at one time or another wonders if they've made a mistake. But my dad always said you can't unscramble an egg."

"Unscramble an egg? I like that. I remember your dad. Was it Hawkins?"

"Hankins. And he liked you a lot."

"So, what went wrong? Did I do something to drive you away?"

"No, not at all. When you're a kid, what do you know about life? I sure didn't know much."

"Will, there's some nice places to go to in Crooked Creek. I mean, if you want to go."

"I want to bad, but I won't. Carla, I've never walked a crooked line in all my married days."

"Well, if nobody agrees on what's a straight line, how do you know when a line is crooked?"

"You know, Carla. Nobody has to tell you. You just know."

"Now, that's a good answer. There's plenty of guys who want to be with me. Unfortunately, none of them would have answered that question the same way. Will, go home to your wife and stay home."

Chapter Twenty-Two

When Jesse drove up Fancy Hollow, he expected to see Ollie sitting on the front porch waiting for him. Jesse wanted to avoid Thalia if possible and started to turn his truck around when she opened the door and waved for him to come back.

It was warm inside the cabin and the smell of ink, wood smoke, and apple pie mingled in the air. Thalia removed a fresh-baked apple pie from the oven and said, "Jesse, every time I bake a pie, you manage to show up. How do you do it?"

"The Bible says the Lord works in mysterious ways."

"The Lord has more important things on His mind than you eating apple pie."

"Where did Ollie go? I was supposed to pick him up today."

"Have a seat. Ollie went to the hardware store for more nails."

"Thalia, how soon do you have to be out?"

"Clive McAlister is giving us until late summer. That's good in a way, but Ollie's sure to find out sooner or later. I swear, it seems like families fall apart after they give up their land."

"I see it happening more and more. So many of our young people are heading north to the factories."

"Just look at our neighbors, the Callahan's. They sold their land, and now the youngest boy is in the army, the girl is married and living in Texas, and the oldest boy is working in Detroit. The whole family hasn't been together in ten years."

"I can't imagine Ollie not living in Fancy Hollow."

"I remember when I was a little girl, some families owned fifty, even sixty acres. Now It's all gone. People are lucky if they have two or three acres left. Will says we mountain people are our own worst enemies because we fight change so much. Maybe he's right."

"I'll talk to Ollie after Will talks to him."

"I want Ollie to go back to school. The community college the state opened in Cumberland is the best thing to ever happen to Harlan County."

"The second best thing. You're the best thing to ever happen to Harlan County."

"Jesse Collins, that may be the nicest thing you've ever said to me."

"Thalia, I need to tell you something before Ollie gets back. It's very important. So please listen carefully. I've signed my house and property over to you and Ollie."

"I knew Deacon Cartwright would eventually run you crazy. But why would you do such a foolish thing? Please don't tell me you're leaving Harlan County."

"It's time for me to move on. Besides, Ollie needs land, and I've got eight acres. But it has to remain a secret between you two. I don't want Will thinking I'm undermining his marriage."

"He's done that all by himself. But if you leave, where would you go? What would you do?"

"Thalia, I have to get away from Harlan County, and you know why?"

"No, I don't know why. You've never told me anything. But I'll do it on one condition. Tell me how you feel about me."

"I don't know what you mean?"

"Don't be coy with me. I can see right through you."

"What good would it do? You're a married woman, and we shouldn't talk like this."

"You speak such beautiful words about honesty, character, and living with a purpose. Either you're phony or afraid of me. Which is it?"

"I don't have the right to tell you anything. I gave that up long ago. Besides, nothing would change."

"What you don't know about women, I could write a book."

"You belong to someone else."

"Jesse Collins, if I had my rifle, I'd shoot you in the rear end."

"You don't know what you're asking."

"Believe me, I know. Look me in the eyes and tell me I never meant anything to you."

"Thalia, please."

"What's that you preach all the time about truth-the truth shall set you free."

"Please, don't."

"Tell me that you hate me or that you don't care one way or the other. It would be easier than not knowing. That's all I'm asking and nothing more."

"Thalia, once you let the hogs out of the pen, you can't get them back in so easy."

"Is that the best you can do? Hogs in a pen? You talk about love like you have a glass wall surrounding you."

"You know how I feel about you. There's no need for words."

"Jesse, you're a coward. Maybe you're like someone who talks about the joy of singing when they've never sung in their life."

"Thalia, why are you hurting me like this?"

"Jesse, I can't stand for anyone to hurt you. I have to bite my tongue when I hear that loudmouth Cartwright running you down. But I can't live without knowing. Don't you need to know that you're loved just for who you are? Don't you need that, Jesse? Oh, Jesse, please tell me."

"Thalia, you're right about the truth setting you free. But the truth is a sharp knife that cuts deep. Every feeling doesn't need to be spoken to be true."

"Do you want me to tell you how I feel about you?"

"Good Lord, no."

"Then you better open your heart and speak the truth. If not, I just might show up Sunday morning and sit on the front row. I'll wear my prettiest dress and hat and stand up and testify how I feel about the pastor."

"Is that a threat?"

"It's a threat, a promise, a pledge. Call it what you want. You've got a decision to make. Jesse, it's your last chance to speak with me. Otherwise, we'll not speak again, even to say hello."

"Thalia, I can't lose your friendship. It means too much to me."

"Then speak your piece now, or you won't be welcome in this house again. That's all I've got to say."

When the sun sliced through the mist and crept into the cabin, minute dust particles began to dance and prance in the sunlight. For several minutes neither spoke. It was like the brief interlude, almost sacred silence before a dynamite blast ripped tons of coal loose from the earth's grasp.

Suddenly, Jesse clasped Thalia's hands and emitted a gut-wrenching squall that can only flow from a tortured soul. He jerked his hands away and pounded the table with both fists, and looked into Thalia's direct, unblinking gaze. Tears streaked his face. He spoke so softly Thalia could barely hear him.

"Thalia, I've never loved anyone like I love you. Sometimes, I go walking in the middle of the night, fall on my knees, look up at God's heaven, and swear I'd cut off my right arm if I could do things over again. Last week, I dreamed about you again. I dreamed that we were young and courting. The dream was so real I hated opening my eyes that morning. If I could turn back time, it'd do it in a minute."

"Oh, Jesse, why did you throw it all away?"

"I told you before I thought I could see my shadow move like it's got a will of its own. I believe that's a part of me outside my body searching, trying to grab hold of what I've lost. I feel for people who don't understand that God's greatest gift to us is love. Yet we squander it, trample it beneath our feet. God, forgive us."

"No more, Jesse. Say no more."

"Do you remember the revival last year? The church was full for three straight nights. The last night of the revival, I couldn't sleep, so I got up at two o'clock and walked the night. It started pouring rain, but I just kept walking. I said your name over and over again. Come dawn, I was standing at my door. I had no idea how I got there."

"Jesse, it's too much. I can't bear it."

"Now, here's the strange part. I was sick in bed for three days, and you came to take care of me. But how could you know I was sick? God sent an angel disguised as you to nurse me. Even if you were a thousand miles away, your soul and spirit were there. God used you to save my life."

"Jesse, this conversation never happened. It's just a dream. Go now and never come back. Please leave Harlan County and start a new life."

"Tell Ollie I can't work at the Wooten's house today. I've got a young couple that's having problems. The mothers-in-law don't get along, and it's causing a heap of trouble. What God joins together, let no man put asunder. That applies to you and Will and me."

"It never happened, Jesse. It never happened."

Chapter Twenty-Three

Clive McAlister sat at his desk, looking at a folder. He was mystified by the senseless destruction. At first, the property damage was minor and grew increasingly worse. Someone cut a chain-link fence in a dozen places, broke sixteen windows at the company warehouse, and slashed eleven tires on company vehicles. Two days later, a company truck was hot-wired and shoved over a cliff. Vehicle destroyed. A bulldozer was driven into a pond, severely damaging the engine. But the last act was of utmost concern. When someone stole dynamite, powder, blasting caps, and fuses from a concrete bunker, Clive immediately contacted the company's special investigators.

Meanwhile, Ollie Poser had been missing for a week, and Clive was trying to figure out if Ollie was crazy or just plain mean. Clive had a cousin who had struggled with severe depression, and he could sympathize up to a point. Therapy instead of jail time?

Clive slammed down the folder and said, "Will, these two gentlemen work for MMR's security. Thurman Moberly, chief detective, and Burke Whitaker, his assistant. Will, if you have any idea where your son is, please tell them. They can help."

"Have you never heard of innocent until proven guilty? Nobody can prove Ollie's done a darn thing."

The superintendent exhaled, slowly trying to control his temper. He was tired, hungry, and angry. "He's been gone a week," Clive said. "No one knows where he is. Clemon Grover was hunting the other day and saw Ollie cutting toward a ridge back to town."

"Clemon's glasses are thicker than an airplane's windshield. Eyes so bad, he almost shot his brother when they went deer hunting last year."

"Clemon had a pair of binoculars. Besides, you have to admit it looks suspicious with Ollie coming home, grabbing a rifle, and storming out of the house."

"Ollie's a different breed, and he gets that from his mother. Ollie thinks he's another Daniel Boone. He's a throwback to another generation, and in a way, I admire him for that."

"The day Ollie took off, my boy, Sherman, asked him when he was moving to town since his family sold the land. Ollie flew into a rage and threw a cue ball through a poolroom window."

"Is that the way it happened? Ollie and Sherman got into a fight, and Ollie got the best of Sherman. Maybe Sherman figured it was payback."

"The boys made peace and shook hands. They were playing a game of pool that afternoon."

"I knew Ollie would be upset about me selling the land. I should've told him before he found out. But he's gone off by himself before and camped for a few days to blow off steam. He'll hike in the mountains and come back with herbs and plants to sell. I couldn't add up the money he's made over the years selling ginseng."

"Ollie's been gone a week. There's been vandalism for a week. Quite a coincidence, isn't it?"

"Have you thought about that preacher, Jesse Collins? He's been gone for a week. Why isn't he a suspect?"

"Mr. Moberly and Mr. Whitaker take it from here."

Moberly opened his folder, cleared his throat, and awaited a clear signal from the superintendent before speaking. Meanwhile, Whitaker squirmed in his seat, champing at the bit, looking too eager. Clive nodded for Moberly to begin.

"Ollie Poser is almost seventeen and a high school dropout. The superintendent threatened to suspend him unless he told who stole test finals in history, biology, and science. The superintendent knows Ollie saw the culprits but refused to inform on them."

"Please continue," McAlister said a bit impatiently.

"Ollie has no record of arrests even though he was picked up twice for drinking in public. He wasn't intoxicated, so the police let him off with a warning. He's been in three fistfights this past year, but witnesses said he wasn't the instigator in any of the fights."

"This is interesting but cut to the chase."

"He's a loner, a bit high strung, and someone, when provoked, might commit acts of violence. And he seems to have an almost fanatical attachment to his land."

"Mr. Whitaker, tell us about Jesse Collins and make it brief. I have a meeting in an hour."

"He's the pastor at Flatgap Baptist Church. He's an excellent boxer but is a peace-loving man. We've interviewed a lot of his church members, and only one thinks he is capable of violence."

"Has he been gone a week?"

"Correct. And Jesse's four-wheel-drive truck is missing. Collins told his church members he needed some time off. He left the day after Ollie took off."

"Sum it up quickly, Mr. Whitaker."

"Collins worked in the mines for eight years before suffering a work-related injury. He threatened to sue the company and received an out-of-court settlement."

"What about his politics?"

"It's hard to get a handle on him. He's something of a loner. Never been married, doesn't date. His faith is the priority in his life. Also, Collins has remained neutral about people selling their land. He doesn't discuss politics from the pulpit. And he doesn't express support or opposition to coal mining."

"We could've made better use of this time. Find Collins and Poser, and please use restraint. Will, if you know anything, now is the time to speak."

"I've had my say."

After Will, Moberly, and Whitaker left his office, Clive again looked at the file. How in the world did someone get in the bunker? He had dealt with problems like this before. But this time, he was worried. He opened his desk drawer, inspected his pistol, and told himself he better kept it loaded and the safety off.

Around five p.m., Gladys, his loyal and hard-working secretary, left for the day. He stood, stretched, and looked out his office windows with the view of the valley below. His wife had begged him to retire last year. He told himself he better start listening to her advice. He locked his file cabinet, desk drawers, and office door. He decided to leave the lights on in Gladys' office. As he drove his Jeep down the hill to Hoedown, he said aloud, "I'm going to give Gladys a raise."

Chapter Twenty-Four

If Hankins arose at dawn, he would be snoring in his rocking chair two hours later, making him wonder why he did not stay in bed a little longer. Ollie joked that Hankins had rocked so many miles it would take him half-way to Lexington.

This morning he fell asleep with a letter in his hand. It was from Jasper, and Hankins read it three times. Hankins would share the news with Will when the time was right. Jasper even ended the letter with, "Dad, I may not act it sometimes, but I love you." Over the years, Jasper had used many four-letter words, often with much enthusiasm and frequency, but not this one. If Hankins remembered correctly, it was only the third letter Jasper had written in his life. The other two had been to his mother.

Dad,

Clete and me are fine. We're both working at the steel mill, but we had enough seniority to get out of the heat. We both got jobs in the warehouse, and it's about thirty-five degrees cooler. But it was a cut in pay for us.

We both drive forklifts, but I caught on quicker than Clete. The men are scared to get near him when he's driving a fork-

lift. The boss said if Clete dropped one more thing, he was going back in the heat.

The problem is Clete's mind is on a woman named Donna Wheat. How's that for a dang name? Clete said, "Don't tell you nothing in case things don't work out." Donna's never been married and just turned forty. She's sort of plain, but makeup could help. She's got some strange ideas, though. She said men don't wear makeup, so why should a woman? I thought of a good reply, but Clete would of hit me, so I said nothing. But she could make a half-decent wife.

And Donna can sure fry some chicken. She ain't after his money because she's got more than him. Works in the office at the steel mill. Donna has four or five pretty young gals working under her. Besides, it'd take a crowbar to pry Clete's wallet out of his britches. I thought Clete messed up when he said he wouldn't marry anyone unless they knew the Lord. I reckon she's going to church now. Go figure.

Well, Dad, I'm saving the best for last. Donna has a sister name of Sally that can sing better than Patsy Cline. And all she wears is blue jeans, which is fine with me. Sally kind of reminds me of my third wife, but Sally has a peach face and is really plump. The only problem is she's hateful in the morning. I tease her and call her shred-

ded wheat, and she gets really mad and throws things.

Right now, there's just the two of us cause Sally's first husband got custody of their two kids. Sally says the judge was unfair. She says her second husband was paid to testify against her with a bunch of lies and the judge believed them. She thinks her husband's lawyer might've bribed the judge.

But my problem is she won't marry me unless I go to church. Sally said the reason her first two marriages didn't work out was because of no church wedding. So I'll have to get saved, baptized, and married in a church. I hope it don't cost too much. I thought maybe me and Clete could do it together and split the cost, but Donna threw a fit.

Dad, I'll go for now and hit the sack early. I'm awful tired. I'm twelve years older than Sally, and it shows. I never asked anybody to pray for me before, but I am now. They say the third time is charm. In my case, I hope it's the fourth. Clete said to tell you we won't make it home for Christmas, but we'll be home at Easter.

Dad, I may not act it sometimes, but I love you.

Your loyal son, Jasper James Poser.

Hankins had just dozed off again when he heard footsteps treading on the porch. It took Hankins three tries before his chair ejected him in the direction of the door. "Chester, I was hoping you were Ollie."

"Well, unless you're blind, you can see I ain't. But I heard Ollie was in a heap of trouble."

"Have they found him?" Hankins said, now fully awake.

"No, but I ran into Will yesterday. Thalia has just about run herself crazy looking for that boy. She's out looking for him now."

"Lord, have mercy; that's a strong-willed woman."

"Will said she caught him gone, packed her saddlebags, grabbed her rifle, and took off on Biscuit. I reckon that's a horse. Will's so mad he can't see straight."

"He'd have to hogtie Thalia to keep her home. She thinks the sun rises and sets on that boy. Any word about Jesse? Is he still missing?"

"I believe so. But let me tell you what I heard at the barbershop yesterday. Doak Owens told old rusty clippers—that's my barber. I wish he'd sharpen those darn things or get a new pair. He pinches my scalp every time he touches my head."

"Good Lord, Chester. Get on with it."

"Oh yeah. Like I was saying, Doak said the company was offering a reward for information concerning Ollie's whereabouts."

"Folks are always needing money. Somebody will turn him in."

"And here's something else. Doak said the police are watching your house to see if Ollie shows up. Just thought I'd tell you."

"Want some coffee? I'll fix another pot."

"Got to run. I promised to take my brother to the graveyard today. He has to go there at least once a month. I told him it's cold as the dickens and wait until it warms up, but he won't listen."

"It's always something."

"Ain't it, though," Chester said and bit off a plug of tobacco, stuffing it in his already puffy jaws.

Chapter Twenty-Five

The company completed the dam's construction a week ago after months of around-the-clock work. And that was fortunate because the first week of December, the rain pounded the earth. The rain alternated between a heavy downpour and a drizzle, with only an occasional slowdown. The trickling mountain streams fused into a mighty flow, and the dam was slowly filling.

Harley Simpkins, the chief engineer, watched the water flow into the dam. Moberly and Whitaker shook their heads in disbelief. "I've never seen a dam built this good. But will it withstand a flood?" Moberly asked.

Simpkins grinned. "Look, we've installed a concrete spillway for an overflow. Plus, we got discharge pipes two feet from the top. Got a deep clay bottom to prevent seepage."

However, Whitaker was unconvinced. "I've seen some awful bad flooding in my time. And I was always told the dams would hold. I wouldn't want to be sitting in that little church in the valley if this thing broke loose."

"Whitaker, if it weren't for this dam, the valley would already have major flooding. This is a blessing in disguise whether the people know it or not," Simpkins replied.

Moberly laughed. "Ain't much chance of Whitaker sitting in any little church."

"I went to church when I was young. But by eighth-grade, I figured I knew more than the preacher."

"I guess you had better things to do, like drinking, fighting, and stealing. Did I leave anything out?"

"Just the cussing and lying part."

Simpkins was a company man for sure. He could not grasp that anyone would think MRR's presence was anything but heaven-sent for the local people. "If things work out, this company will be here for at least forty years. We're not like those jack-legged coal companies that are here today and gone tomorrow. That's why this dam is so important. You've got to protect the dam at all costs. Do you understand?"

Moberly was getting tired of Simpkins. He knew what was at stake. The company had twelve detectives out policing the hills, and all were armed. "We'll get Poser and Collins. It won't be long," Moberly said.

"I'm going to meet with Mr. McAlister. The minute you catch them, call the dispatcher on your two-way radios. Mr. McAlister wants them brought in peacefully. The company doesn't need any bad press, especially when things are going so well."

After Simpkins left, Whitaker snickered and said, "He ain't got a clue."

Moberly and Whitaker used their field glasses to canvass the area. Almost all the trees, except a few evergreens, had parted with their leaves, making their view extensive.

After fifteen minutes, Whitaker thought he saw something. He adjusted his field glasses to zero in on a pile of brush. He was sure something moved. It was just a speck, but he definitely saw something. As the speck grew larger, he realized it was an outline of a man hunkered down behind a pile of brush.

"Hey, boss, talk a look at that brush pile straight ahead. You see anything?"

Moberly adjusted his glasses repeatedly while shaking his head. "Are you sure you saw movement?"

"I'm positive. Right behind that huge pile of brush."

"Are you positive?"

"Yes! What else do you want me to say?"

"You can drive, and I'll ride shotgun. But remember, the superintendent wants them brought in peacefully. I hope we can avoid a fight."

"Boss, are you getting too old for this rough stuff? You may want to think about retirement."

"I've been thinking about retirement for the past ten years. The closer I get, the farther away it seems."

"I wouldn't mind roughing them up a little before we take them in. Teach those losers a good lesson."

"You don't know much about these people, do you?"

"I know I don't want to spend my life in eastern Kentucky doing this job."

"Treat these people with respect. Talking down to them is the worst thing you can do. And be a good listener. Sometimes people just need to get things off their chests. Listening is a very undervalued talent."

"What if they still want to fight?"

"Then do what you have to do. Now, remember, give Collins and Poser a chance to surrender. They may be tired and hungry. Do you understand?"

"I understand this will look good on my resume. We both might get a promotion or a bonus. Then I can get out of here and get to where I belong."

"And where's that?"

"Anywhere but here."

Chapter Twenty-Six

Thalia searched the steep hills and back trails, hoping to catch a glimpse of Ollie. But where could he be? Thalia had left home two days ago and was now out of food and water. Thalia wished she had brought more grain for her horse. Thalia stopped to rest Biscuit, and her mare seemed to be more tired and hungry than her. Thalia found two apples in her saddlebags, and Biscuit did short work of both. The only thing Thalia had left was a piece of peppermint candy. Biscuit loved peppermint and nudged Thalia repeatedly, wanting more.

It was only an hour's slow ride to the cabin, but Thalia decided to take a different path back home to try and find her son. Thalia decided to stop and rest a spell. She sat down under a huge oak tree, laid her head back and fell asleep, and dreamed snapshots of her past.

In her dream, time and reality had no meaning. Thalia awoke at dawn in an unfamiliar house that was cold. Thalia sat up in bed and pulled a heavy quilt up to her chin. Through the windows, she could see a corral where a half-dozen horses were prancing around, breathing the frosty air.

There was a man in the house. Could the man be her husband? All Thalia knew was that he was supposed to be there. The man had his back to her, placing a log in the fireplace. Outside, snowflakes were swirling and rising and falling as if trying to decide if they should land or not.

The low light blurred the man's face. When he handed Thalia a steaming cup of coffee and fluffed up her pillows, he said, "Stay in bed until the house is warm. I know the cold weather hurts your knee."

He must have known Thalia when she was a teenager. Thalia was sixteen when her dad's horse threw her after being frightened by a fieldmouse running across a horse trail. Her knee ached in damp, rainy, and cold weather. Every few years, the pain, although infrequent, increased in intensity.

When Thalia looked out the window again, the entire landscape was painted white with snow. But Thalia would not get out of bed yet. The man sat on the side of her bed and began brushing her long, tangled hair. She giggled and wondered what kind of man would do such a thing? But he was the same man that had cut a mountain of firewood, replaced the roof on the barn, and planted a garden that was the envy of all the neighbors who came to visit. She felt warm and safe and loved.

Thalia yawned, stretched, and said she would get up and fix breakfast. But the man told her to stay in bed until she drank a second cup of coffee. He must know her well. She always wanted two cups of coffee before she did anything. But how did he know?

When Thalia was eighteen, her mother, also named Thalia, had finally succumbed after a long illness. This same man had stood with her at the gravesite. On the way to the family cemetery, the sky contemptuously began to spit snow and turned the road leading to the gravesite into a treacherous mush. Several cars in the funeral procession got stuck in the thick mud and turned back.

As Thalia and the man stood around the open grave, a frigid wind rushed down the hollow and caused the tent covering the grave to flap wildly. The arrogant wind swayed Thalia's body, and she would have fallen had he not gripped her tightly, keeping her steady on her feet.

She looked out the window again and saw two people in a canoe, going around in circles. They finally got the hang of paddling and made it to shore and sat on a log by a sandy riverside. He asked her if she had been afraid. She thought about it a long time before saying she did not know what the word meant. He laughed and said it was not a real word. It was a word people made up to confuse people who loved each other. He said people were always trying to pull them apart. She would never forget his words. "But hell can't stand against a man and a woman who are best friends."

"Have you always loved me?" she said.

"I loved you before you were you."

"But why do you speak in riddles?"

"Because I am a riddle," he said and began laughing.

Thalia asked the man his name, and he said he did not know his name. Thalia said, "Why can't I see your face?"

"Because I can't see my face," he answered.

Thalia closed her eyes again, and another scene from the past came into focus. The day after she graduated high school, Thalia decided to go horseback riding. Her dad said to travel the long winding road and always take the right turn.

"You mean, take the path that goes to the right?"

"No, I mean, take the correct path."

So Thalia traveled along the winding horse trail, and over and over again, the trail forked. Thalia decided to let the horse pick the fork to travel. After many hours, Thalia ended up back where she had started. "Did I do right?" Thalia asked her dad. "Did I make the correct turn every time?"

Her father replied, "My dear precious daughter, the farther you travel, the closer you are to where you started."

Another memory tumbled from the past. It was Thalia's birthday, and she received many presents. But she had wanted only one gift. The floor was piled high with a hundred presents of every size and shape imaginable. Thalia picked up present after present, unable to find the right one.

In frustration, Thalia asked some young man which present actually belonged to her. But he only smiled. She became frantic and began to open every present, but it was never the right one.

The man laughed and said, "The presents are all the same, and yet they are different."

Finally, she opened the last present, and there was another box inside that one. Then another and another, until only a tiny box big enough to hold a ring was left. She gleefully opened the last box, and specks of light flew into the air. The specks merged to form a beam of light so bright she shielded her eyes. The light filled the room and grew in intensity and then exploded. When she turned to look at the man, he was gone.

Thalia awoke when Biscuit started making a noise and stamping her hooves. Thalia again heard a booming noise. Gradually, she realized the explosion was only thunder, and a storm was on the way. "Biscuit, we better get away from this tree and head home," Thalia said. Biscuit stamped her front hooves in approval.

Chapter Twenty-Seven

A branch snapped, and Ollie swung around and pointed his rifle at Jesse. "Preacher, I almost shot you. What are you doing here, anyway?" Ollie has been stringing a fuse to ignite the dynamite.

"Ollie, if you blow the dam, they'll hunt you down, and you may get killed. Your mother would never get over it. Please don't hurt her."

"The coal companies destroy everything. They always have, and they always will. Somebody's got to do something about it."

"The company legally owns the land. And they plan to hire five hundred miners immediately. Just think how much it will help the people here."

"God, you're naïve. They'll start mining underground but give them a few years, and it'll be all strip-mining. There won't be a tree left in Harlan County unless I stop them."

"If there are no mines, where will the people work? They can't make moonshine."

"Why not? I hear you did."

"I've done a lot of things I'm not proud of doing."

"Was running off and leaving Mom one of them?"

Jesse made a sudden move, and Ollie aimed the rifle at him. "Don't force me to shoot you. I shot that company Jeep over a hundred yards away. I shot two tires, and when the fools turned around, I shot the other two. But I didn't shoot them."

"Ollie, you don't want to hurt anyone. I know you feel betrayed, but there's a right way to resolve this. I've made a will, and I've signed my house and land over to you and your mom. You have land. Eight acres."

"You're crazy. Why would you give your land away? Wait a minute. You still love my mom, don't you? That's it! That's it!"

"Remember when you hunted on my property last year? You said it was the most pheasant and grouse you've ever seen."

How could Ollie make Jesse understand how he felt? Ollie had never put much store in a sermon, but he remembered when Jesse preached on the twenty-third psalm about lying down in green pastures. Jesse said God commanded people to love and care for God's creation. That was one of the few thing's Jesse ever said that made sense. Jesse could not understand that Ollie was a part of the land, and the land was a part of him.

Ollie could remember when he was a child and families had a reunion, and at least sixty-seventy people would show up and stay for days. Family meant something then. But after the people broke up the land, things started to change. The kids inherited a few acres here and there, but they stopped farming, and only a few people even bothered to plant a garden. Not long afterward, the kids sold their few acres and moved from eastern Kentucky or relocated to a dreary mining camp. Now, they shopped at the company store.

And once the land no longer belonged to a family, something they had no name for was lost and could never be regained. When enough time passed, they forgot the thing existed.

Back when people grew their food, they looked at life differently. They loaded their trucks with stuff from their gardens, drove to town, and sold it so cheap they almost gave it away. But it was a way to be a part of something. No one could destroy it from the outside, only from the inside. And that is what happened.

Ollie remembered when their family had company-back when his dad enjoyed visitors. Before they left, his mom would send him to the garden and pick a dozen ears of corn, tomatoes, green beans, a peck of potatoes, or whatever else was in the garden. Now, the same people shopped at the company store, and they hardly spoke to each other. They could not look each other in the eye. Were they ashamed of what they let happen?

How could he make Jesse understand? When a family lived on the land for generations, there was a spirit that dwelled there. Not like a ghost or something silly like that. But the land would speak to you. If you had a hundred acres and sold off a little at a time, you cut out a piece of the heart. Finally, the land died, and things stopped growing. That was why the soil was so poor in parts of the county.

Ollie could recall when he was twelve, he found an unopened bottle of bourbon hidden in a closet his dad was saving for a special occasion. Ollie could not resist taking a sip. But every time he took a sip, he refilled the bottle with water. After a year, it was nothing but colored water. When his dad finally took a drink, he almost gagged. Will laid the switch to Ollie for that. But it was the same way with the land. The land was diluted so much there was nothing left: no heart, no spirit, no soul.

Ollie decided to act. He looked through his field glasses, chuckled, and handed them to Jesse. Moberly and Whitaker were limping in the distance. "One is limping with his right leg, the other with his left. If you put the two of them together, you might make a decent man, but I doubt it," Ollie chuckled.

When Ollie took another look through his glasses, Jesse grabbed at a pistol Ollie had removed from his jacket pocket. Ollie fired a shot that barely grazed Jesse's right shoulder. Ollie then kneeled and lit the fuse. It took a third try with the lighter's flickering flame before the fuse caught fire.

"Jesse, get up there behind those rocks. I hope you ain't hurt bad. Mom would skin me alive if I did hurt you. Don't worry about me telling Dad what we talked about. But a blind man could see how much you care for Mom."

The explosion ripped a twelve-foot wide hole in the dam, and water poured through the opening, roaring down the narrow valley, felling small trees and tumbling boulders like marbles. However, the dam held.

"I don't believe it. I used enough dynamite to blow up two dams. What went wrong?"

"Ollie, it's not like in the movies."

"Guess I'll have to do it again."

Ollie and Jesse squalled when the entire center of the dam collapsed a few seconds later, and a river roared down the valley and lifted the small church like a child playing with a toy and set it on higher ground.

"The church didn't break apart. I can't believe it," Jesse shouted.

Ollie laughed and said, "You reckon I used enough dynamite after all?"

"I can't believe it. The water set the church down on the level ground where it should've been built in the first place."

Ollie looked through his glasses again and said, "They'll be here any minute. The fools are limping fast."

"Ollie, get out of here. Now."

Ollie looked through the scope of his rifle. Did he plan to shoot them or just fire a warning shot? Ollie grew careless and underestimated the hand speed of Jesse, who was twenty-seven years older. Jesse snatched the rifle and threw it on the ground. Ollie lunged for the gun, but Jesse, despite his wounded shoulder, struck Ollie with a right, left, then right, and gently eased Ollie to the ground.

He searched Ollie's pockets and found a lighter, several feet of fuse, three blasting caps, and a pocketknife. A minute later, Moberly and Whitaker limped frantically up the hill and pointed a rifle and a shotgun at Jesse.

Moberly yelled, "You fools! Why? Why? Are you people so stupid you can't see we're trying to do something that will benefit everybody? If you people had your way, we'd be back in the stone age. Whitaker, handcuff Collins and check out that idiot on the ground. Collins, what in God's name is wrong with you?"

"I've been cranky since I quit smoking."

Whitaker shoved Jesse and said, "I'll show you cranky." He slapped Jesse several times and then spit in his face.

"Whitaker, that's enough. He's trying to provoke you. Can Ollie stand? Did a rock hit him or what?"

"Boss, the blast should've blown his head off."

Moberly scowled and said, "Jesse, why did you and Poser do it? Make a clean break, and it might go easier on you? Was it a personal vendetta against the coal company? Go ahead and get it off your chest."

Whitaker had handcuffed Jesse, and Jesse was already cramping. "Alright. Ollie caught me lighting a fuse and tried to stop me, and we fought. You can see the results."

Moberly frowned when Whitaker moved toward Jesse. "No, let him talk," Moberly said.

"I didn't want a dam built at the mouth of the hollow above my church, so I blew it up. Check my pockets, and you'll see the evidence."

Are you trying to tell me that Poser had nothing to do with any of this?"

"At first, I was going to frame him. I knew he was upset about his dad selling off their land. I figured you'd blame him for what happened, too."

"What else did you do?"

"Lot of other things. Too much to mention."

"You tell us, wise guy," Whitaker said.

"If I told you, Whitaker, you'd just forget. You don't look real bright to me. You're so slow I can't even get mad at you."

"I'm warning you, smart mouth."

"Whitaker, I heard you quit sixth grade because you hated recess."

"Keep it up. Nothing I'd like better than to bust a hillbilly's hard head."

"Whitaker, you'll never make it to retirement. You'll end up spending the rest of your life using a shovel because you're too dumb to operate mining equipment."

Whitaker became enraged are struck Jesse with his fist. Jesse shook off the blow and rammed his shoulder into Whitaker's stomach. The impact knocked Whitaker back against a rock, causing him to strike his head. Jesse took off running surprisingly fast for someone who had their hands cuffed behind their back.

Moberly attempted to chase Jesse but stopped in his tracks. "Collins, you're a poor excuse for a preacher. Whitaker, are you hurt bad? We'll catch Collins and take him to the police station when the other detectives get here. Now get that idiot Poser on his feet."

Whitaker struggled to stand, grabbed Ollie's rifle, and aimed at Jesse, who was almost out of range in a gathering of trees. He fired two shots into Jesse's back. Jesse stumbled forward a few more yards before collapsing. Moberly jerked the rifle from Whitaker and threw it as far as he could. Whitaker stumbled backward, fell to the ground, and held his head.

"You fool! You miserable fool! Am I the only sane man on this mountain? Do you want a guilty man to go free? He was lying to protect Poser for some reason. Whitaker, you just resigned, whether you know or not. But don't leave town. You have a lot to explain to the police."

Chapter Twenty-Eight

Food graced the table in the Poser cabin, but no one was eating. Thalia looked out the windows, Will stared at his coffee cup, Hankins read his Bible, and Ollie laid his head on the table. Although Jesse died the day before, somehow, a part of him still hovered in the air. A spirit began to move about the room, touching, challenging, consoling.

The Flatgap Baptist Church deacons, intimidated by Deacon Cartwright, voted three to two against burying Jesse in the church cemetery. Will finally broke the long afternoon silence and said, "What's wrong with the town cemetery? It's not like Jesse will complain about it."

Thalia gritted her teeth and clenched her fists while struggling to speak. "He'll be buried here."

"You think I'm blind?" Will said. "You think I don't know?"

"You don't know anything. Jesse was good. Just plain good."

"Yeah, he was so good a lot of his church members turned their backs on him. And you making a scene like you did. I'm ashamed to visit that church again."

"No doubt, you'll be missed."

"If you'd just slapped Deacon Cartwright, but you throw a punch like a prizefighter. Who taught you to punch like that? Well, never mind."

Thalia believed some church members were quick to abandon Jesse because he challenged them to be more like

Jesus. Thalia thought if Jesus walked inside Flatgap Baptist Church, Deacon Cartwright would ask him where he got all those strange notions. Why did people look for heaven so high up and so far away they could not bear a little bit of heaven on earth?

Ollie had remained quiet all day, barely able to speak. He wondered how people could love Jesse one week and reject him the next. But they did not know that Jesse had taken his place.

Hankins finally spoke and said, "Jesse should be buried here."

"Dad, you be quiet. You have no say in this matter."

"Will, you an ignorant man. The more you learn, the less you understand," Hankins snapped back.

Ollie leaped from the table and said, "I feel like Jesse's here and trying to tell us something."

"Ollie, don't fall apart of me now," Will said.

"I've got to get it off my chest. I've got to confess to the police," Ollie continued.

"What good would come of it?" Will said. "Nobody knows the truth but us, and it's going to stay that way."

Thalia spoke softly, "A part of me wants Ollie to confess. But a part of me feels if we bury Jesse here, we can move on. It's a way to honor him for what he's done for this family. Will, if you can't see it, then you're a fool."

"Don't talk to me like that. Who do you think you are?"

"A wife who sees her husband clearly for the first time in her life."

"Ollie, are you going to let your mother talk to me that way?"

"Dad, I love you, but I haven't liked you in years."

"What would people think if we buried Jesse in the family cemetery?"

Thalia said, "Who cares what anyone thinks? Our son is free because of him. He died for Ollie. Why can't you see that?"

Ollie prided himself on never crying. But now, he began to cry softly. "Why did he did it? Why did Jesse take my place? It don't make no sense."

Will's hardened exterior was beginning to crack, but he feared his family might perceive any kindness as a weakness. "Ollie, he took your place because he, he loved your mother. He loved your mother. He's always loved her!"

Thalia tried to remain strong, but now tears rolled down her cheeks. "Yes, Will, Jesse loved me, but not in the way you think. Jesse looked past people's meanness and flaws and saw them the way heaven sees them-weak, scared, foolish, but still worth loving. Were all worth loving. Even you, Will."

Will stomped to the pantry and retrieved his favorite bottle of bourbon and said, "You just don't know."

"You're right, and I'm not sure I want to know you anymore."

"If you only knew."

Hankins stood, lit his pipe, and said, "This family will bury Jesse on the hill. And there's something else we should do. We can make amends by repairing the church."

"Dad, I said stay out of this."

"Son, you got so much anger and bitterness inside, you can't tell good from the bad. But you weren't always like that."

"Granddad, what do you mean? What happened?"

"Will, remember how close we were when you were young?"

"Dad, don't say another word."

"Granddad, what happened to change things? Please tell me!"

"Will, this family's survival at stake. This is your last chance with me. If you have anything worth saying, you better speak," Thalia said.

Hankins said, "I never thought this day would arrive. But it's long overdue."

Will shattered his half-full bottle against the fireplace, and flames leaped from the fire into the air but died down quickly. Will lowered his head and said, "Go ahead, Dad. Just go ahead."

"Son, you have to tell them. If you don't, you'll never be free."

Will leaped to his feet and said, "This family has been living a lie. Hankins Poser is not my real father."

"Good Lord, what are you talking about?" Thalia exclaimed.

Ollie exploded, "You lie. You lied about the land. You lie about everything."

"It's true," Hankins said, choking back tears.

Will sat down again and spoke slowly. "You remember me saying I quit my junior year with a month of high school left. I had an A, three B's, and a C. If I had bothered to study hard, I could've made all A's."

Ollie began to cry, "Why, Dad, why?"

"One day, I went home from school to get a copy of my birth certificate for something. I looked through an old trunk in the closet, found some papers, and discovered that Hankins Poser wasn't my father. I've lived with this lie for years. I lost all feeling for my so-called mother and father. They're liars and frauds."

"Shut your mouth. Don't you dare tarnish the name of your mother! There was never a better wife or mother as good as my Sarah. She was your mother, and I'm your father."

"My father was some man in Cincinnati. Don't know who he is and never cared to find out."

"Anybody can be a birth father, but to be a dad, you have to love and care for your own. I remember when you were little, I couldn't wait to get home from the mines and put you on my knee and sing to you. When I had a bad day at work, I'd think about something you said, and it would cheer me up."

Will stood, grabbed his coat and hat, and started toward the door. "Will, if you leave, I won't be here when you get back," Thalia said. "Hankins, please continue," she added. Will sat back down without removing his coat and hat.

"I remember one time when Will was in first grade, and we bought him a John Wayne lunch box. Will loved cowboys, and he sure loved John Wayne. One day, Will took a red crayon and marked with it all over a wall. Will wore it down to a nub, and I made him sit on the couch for an hour and wouldn't let him play with his toys.

"When we got ready to eat around five-thirty, a neighbor knocked on the door and said Will was at their house. Will had been walking down the street and told the neighbor he was running away from home. Will had packed that lunch box with candy bars, snack cakes, and a can of beer. Sarah and me laughed about that for a week."

"Dad, you saved that lunch box all these years. You gave it to me when I was in first grade. I still have it. One day I plan to give it to my son."

"Will, I have so many wonderful memories of you, your mother, and your brothers."

"Dad, how could you forgive her?"

"How do you judge somebody's entire life by one mistake? What kind of world do we live in where nobody forgives nobody? When we do that, we're playing God. Son, I love you, but I don't know what to say or do to reach you. I don't know. I just don't know."

Silence engulfed the cabin. It had been a cold, damp, and overcast day. Although it was only three in the afternoon, it felt like five o'clock. The sun, intimidated most of the day, began to flex its muscles and peep from behind the clouds. Suddenly, it became a bright ball of light. Shadows traipsed along a wall and disappeared into the ceiling.

Will held his head in his hands and began to sob. It had been years since he had shown any real emotion. The four sensed something has changed. Ollie and Hankins stood and placed their arms around Will. Thalia began to cry, but the pain slowly drained from her face. She felt at peace for the first time in a long time.

There was a spirit of healing in the air. Something flashed outside the windows, and everyone turned to look. It was a small snow-white bird. Ollie came to his mother's side, laid a hand on her shoulder, and spoke. "We can get our tools and go to work at the church. There's a couple of guys over there now."

Thalia said, "I'll pack a picnic basket. We've got enough food to feed half the church. There's a couple of hours of daylight left. You boys can work until you give out."

Hankins relit his pipe, coughed, and said, "I can't play a game of checkers without giving out."

"Don't worry, Grandad. You can sit down and be the boss."

Will stood and grabbed the table, his face conveying something that Thalia had not seen in a long time. He spoke so softly Thalia could barely hear him say, "Thalia, can you forgive me?" Will stopped suddenly, unable to speak further.

"I can, and I do."

"Thalia, where do I begin?"

"At the beginning, Will. At the beginning."

Chapter Twenty-Nine

The month of May birthed a mass of wildflowers that blanketed the steep slopes of Harlan County. All along the mountain ridges, wildflowers stood proudly and waved at passersby as if nature was celebrating.

Poser land now belonged to the coal company except for the family cemetery and a few acres. Less than two hundred yards away, an access road wiggled up a hill to one of the company's numerous mine sites.

Thalia kneeled before Jesse's grave and placed an armful of flowers against the headstone that bore the inscription: "We did not lose Jesse—we know where he is." Thalia prayed and then stood with difficulty. Her right knee was getting worse. A sweet wind caressed her face, but she could have sworn a gentle hand touched her cheek. She felt the presence of someone or something that caused her to tingle all over.

The past six months had brought much change. Thalia was less a tomboy and more feminine. She had cut her long hair, gained weight, and bought new, bright-colored clothes. There was still a wisp of sadness about her, laced with peace and contentment. She was almost happy.

Thalia felt Jesse's presence so strongly she spoke to him without feeling foolish. "Jesse, do you like my new outfit?"

Somehow a voice spoke to her spirit. "Thalia, you grow more beautiful every day."

"But why didn't you tell me before?"

"I did, but not in words."

"Jesse, I could always feel your love, but I just needed you to say it. I remember when Ollie had the flu, and I woke at three a.m. and fixed him chicken soup. Will thought I'd had a nervous breakdown. For some reason, I was worried about Ollie and you. When Ollie's fever broke after three days, somehow, I stopped worrying about you. I knew you were better."

"You were there."

"Jesse, how can your spirit be here, and yet you're gone? I don't understand."

"There are mysteries in death as well as life."

"One minute, I'm happy. The next, I'm sad. How can that be?"

"Thalia, you've discovered that chains are made of paper, and you're breaking them one at a time."

"But why didn't I break them before?"

"Because someone lied and said that chains are made of steel."

"Jesse, I feel the presence of love everywhere."

"Love doesn't end at death; it just seeks another path. Once love exists, it can't be destroyed. Love is a mist, a vapor that can penetrate the heavens and return to earth renewed."

"Jesse, I've got some good news. Ollie's got your house, I mean his house, fixed up. Now he's going to college. He wants to become an architect and return to Harlan County and build houses."

"I'm so proud of him."

"And Clive McAlister kept his promise about selling the camp houses. And the company is going to donate forty acres to build a neighborhood and name it Collins. Can you believe it?"

"I can see the last house being built."

"Now, here's something else that's hard to believe. Will and I go to church in town, and I sing in the choir. Will even goes with me on Wednesday night."

"It's not hard to believe from where I dwell."

"And we're going to marriage counseling. We have to go to Hazard, but it's worth it. Jesse, can I learn to love and trust Will again?"

"Thalia, love returns in the way it's needed most. But if you can't forgive, you can't love. If you can't love, you can't feel. If you can't feel, you'll sleepwalk until it's too late. It's up to you and Will."

"Jesse, your church members demanded that you be buried in the church cemetery, and the deacons backed down. And this will shock you. Deacon Cartwright came home one Sunday night after church, and his wife was sitting at the kitchen table. She'd been gone nine years."

"I told her to go home."

"Jesse, why did you have to leave? Wasn't there some other way?"

"Thalia, I'm still in the dark about a lot of things."

"Jesse, I can't come back again."

"I know, Thalia."

"Goodbye, Jesse."

"Goodbye, Thalia."

As Thalia left the cemetery, she began to hum softly. When she passed a tree and heard birds singing, she burst forth in song:

> *Whenever I hear the church bells ring,*
> *Oh, my spirit soars, and I joyfully sing*
> *And I breathe a little heaven on earth*
> *Because I know what I'm truly worth*

Suddenly, birds began to sing from every tree on the hillside. Thalia threw back her head and laughed as the singing escorted her down the hill and safely on her way.

THE END